THE GREATEST WAR

Kamesh Ramakrishna

EPISODES FROM THE MAHABHARATA OF VEDA VYAASA

KASHI PUBLISHING   CAMBRIDGE MA

Amazon KDP ISBN: 978-1521354-82-7

Softcover ISBN (Kashi): 978-1-939338-07-5
USA Retail Price: US$12.99
Copyright © 2015 – 2017 Kamesh Ramakrishna
URL: www.thelastkaurava.com
Discussion: www.facebook.com/kameshramakrishna
Email: Kamesh@kashipub.com

 First US Edition published on September 2017 in the United States
by
Kashi Publishing
Cambridge, MA 02139, USA
Telephone: +1-617-335-1520
Email: publisher@kashipub.com

Disclaimer: This is a work of fiction based on an ancient Hindu epic. Names, characters, places, and incidents are based on the original stories from the Mahabharata. All changes are products of the author's imagination. Any resemblance to actual persons, living or dead, is entirely coincidental. The Views expressed in this book are those of the Author and not those of the Publishers.

Illustrations: Junuka Deshpande
Front Cover photo of a statue is public domain from Creative Commons

Typeset in Palatino Linotype

For my parents

Table of Contents

PREFACE

Most people of Indian or South Asian origin are familiar with the stories and the characters from the Mahabharata. A brief introduction suffices to set the context when narrating an episode. Such an approach would be opaque, if not disconcerting, to most Western readers encountering this material for the first time. The following is a synopsis of the epic.

The *Mahabharata*[1] is the story of a Great War (*Mahā*: Great; *bhāra*[2]: *War*) fought between two sets of cousins vying for the family's kingdom of *Hastinapura*[3]. The winners, the *Pandava*[4]-s (sons of Pandu[5]), consisting of five brothers and *Draupadi*[6], their wife-in-common, endured much abuse from their hundred *Kaurava*[7] (descendants of Kuru) cousins before the final battle that engaged all corners of South Asia. The war ends with almost two million dead warriors, and much sorrow to share. The message that "War is Hell" is emphasized *ad nauseam*.

Krishna[8], who in later times was considered an incarnation of the god Vishnu, is a major figure in the Mahabharata – a cousin to both sides, he acts as a non-fighting charioteer and advisor to the

---

[1] Phonetic: Mahābʰārəta, Syllabic: Mu(d)-ha-bah-rut-u(h).
The conventions followed for spelling names is described in the "Glossary of Names" which also provides a brief reminder of the people or places named. The first occurrence of each name is italicized and accompanied by a pronunciation footnote. A "syllabic" pronunciation is provided to guide readers who do not know the International Phonetic script. Each syllable of the name is described by an equivalent English syllable used in an English word or fragment with the unpronounced part of the word within parenthesis. For example, the "Ma" in Mahabharata is pronounced as the "Mu" in "Mud". The "d" is not pronounced. So the first syllable "Ma" of "Mahabharata" is shown as "Mu(d)" in this example. The full word would be "Mu(d)-hah-bah-rut-u(h)".
[2] Many commentators have translated Mahabharata as "the great story of Bharata's dynasty". That *bhaara* means war (*bharato nama samgrama*) first came to my attention in a report on a paper by Professor M. G. Dhadphale of the Bhandarkar Oriental Research Institute (BORI) presented at the Mahabharata Seminar held in February 2007. I have not been able to get a copy of the paper, but this translation is more cogent than the common one.
[3] Phonetic: Həstināpūrə, Syllabic: Hus(tle)-thin-a(h)-poo(l)-r
[4] Phonetic: Pāṇḍəvə, Syllabic: Pa-unde(r)-vu(h). Generically, Pandava means "descendent of Pandu", in this usage it refers to Pandu's sons.
[5] Phonetic: Pāṇḍu, Syllabic: Pa-unde(r)-oo
[6] Phonetic: Draupədī, Syllabic: Thee-(c)row(d)-pu(s)-thee; Means "Daughter of Drupada"
[7] Phonetic: Kaurəvə, Syllabic: Cow-ru(h)-vu(h)
[8] Phonetic: Kṛṣṇə, Syllabic: Krish-nu(h)

Pandavas.

The Mahabharata war is usually considered mythical. The war described in it is most likely mythical – there are no archaeological discoveries that substantiate a war of the described scale and extent. Astronomical evidence internal to the epic has been used to indicate dates that range from before 3000 BCE to about 1200 BCE. References to foreign countries are either inconsistent or incredible – for instance, a *Yavana*[9] (Ionian Greek?) people residing in a region of modern Afghanistan participate in the war. What is clear is that an oral tradition was put down in writing, possibly between 400 BCE (or earlier) and 400 ACE, and in the process the story was substantially modified. This written-down Mahabharata exists in multiple, slightly varying versions in different parts of India and a critical edition was produced in 1970 by the Bhandarkar Oriental Research Institute of Pune after fifty years of scholarly work.

In 1971, Professor J. A. B. van Buitenen of the University of Chicago began translating the critical edition, but could only complete up to Book 5 and the Bhagavad Gita, before he passed away. This work has been re-started recently and Books 12 onwards have been published, skipping the Books of the war. Meanwhile Penguin (India) has published a complete translation in ten books by Bibek Debroy.

A Summary of the Epic

Shantanu[10], the king of Hastinapura[11], a small kingdom north of modern Delhi on the west bank of the Ganga wants to marry the fisher-girl *Satyavati*, but cannot meet her father's extreme demands. His son *Devavrata*[12], born of his first wife Ganga, makes the marriage possible by giving up his (and his children's) birth-right as heir apparent. He further vows to live a celibate life so that he would not inadvertently have a child who might not accept his sacrifice or his promise to keep Satyavati's descendants on the throne. This self-sacrifice leads to the name by which Devavrata is known in the rest of the epic – *Bhishma*[13]

---

[9] Phonetic: Yəvənə, Syllabic: Ye(n)-vu(h)-nu(h)
[10] Phonetic: Śāṃtənu, Syllabic: Shawn-ton-oo(h)
[11] Phonetic: Həstināpūrə, Syllabic: Hus(tle)-thin-op-oor
[12] Phonetic: Dévəvrətə, Syllabic: They-vu(h)-v-rut-u(h)
[13] Phonetic: Bhīshmə, Syllabic: Bee-shhh-mu(h)

(the *Terrible*, but also *awe-inspiring, beyond the pale, etc.*). For the rest of his long life, Devavrata/Bhishma is Protector of the Realm and thrice, he is the Regent, supporting Satyavati's descendants. He creates an implacable enemy in *Amba*[14], the princess of Kashi[15], when he abducts her sisters to be wives for his half-brother *Vichitravirya*[16]. Vichitravirya has two sons, *Dhritarashtra*[17] and *Pandu*. The older Dhritarashtra is disqualified from inheriting the throne because he is blind; Pandu becomes king but is cursed to die if he engages in sexual activity, making it impossible for him to have children by his wives *Kunti*[18]and *Mādri*[19]. Kunti's knowledge of a magic spell that compels a god to father a child is put to use – Pandu asks her to have three sons, *Yudhishthira*[20], *Bhima*[21], and *Arjuna*[22], by the gods *Dharma*[23], *Vāyu*[24], and *Indra*[25] respectively; Madri has two sons, *Nakula* [26]and *Sahadeva*[27], by the twin gods, the *Aśvins*[28]. After twelve years of abstinence, Pandu attempts to make love to Madri and dies. Madri kills herself out of remorse, leaving all five Pandavas in Kunti's care. Meanwhile, Dhritarashtra marries a princess of *Gandhāra*[29] (a part of modern Afghanistan) who binds her eyes in a show of solidarity with him. They have a hundred children, jointly called Kaurava, also the plural, but we will use the English plural form "Kauravas"). The oldest, *Duryōdhana*[30] is a year younger than Yudhishthira.

Yudhishthira is therefore in line to be the next king. Duryodhana is jealous of the Pandavas and plots to obtain the throne. A series of episodes illustrate the growing discord between the cousins culminating in the attempted murder of the Pandavas and their

---

[14] Phonetic: Əmbā, Syllabic: (H)um-baa
[15] Phonetic: Kāśī, Syllabic: Ka-she
[16] Phonetic: Vicitrəvīryə, Syllabic: We-chit-ru(n)-were(wolf)-ya(h)
[17] Phonetic: Dhṛtərāṣṭrə, Syllabic: Dri(nk)-th(ick)-ra(h)-shh-tru(h)
[18] Phonetic: Kuṃtī, Syllabic: Cou(ld)-nth-e
[19] Phonetic: Mādrī, Syllabic: Ma-dree
[20] Phonetic: Yudhiṣṭhirə, Syllabic: You-dish-tea-ru(h)
[21] Phonetic: Bhimə, Syllabic: Beam-u(h)
[22] Phonetic: Arjunə, Syllabic: Urge-oon-a(h)
[23] Phonetic: Đərmə, Syllabic: The-r-mu(h)
[24] Phonetic: Vāyu, Syllabic: Wa(h)-you
[25] Phonetic: Indrə, Syllabic: Ind-ru(h)
[26] Phonetic: Nəkulə, Syllabic: (K)nuck-oo-lu(h)
[27] Phonetic: Səhədévə, Syllabic: Su(h)-hear(d)-they-vu(h)
[28] Phonetic: Əśvin, Syllabic: (H)ush-win
[29] Phonetic: Gəndārə, Syllabic: Gun-thar-u(h)
[30] Phonetic: Duryōdənə, Syllabic: Th-uri-yo-the-nu(h)

mother. The Pandavas escape into hiding and go to the kingdom of *Panchala*[31] – the wedding choice ceremony of Draupadi, the daughter of *Drupada*[32], king of Panchala results in her unconventional marriage to all five Pandavas. Panchala, on the east bank of the Ganga downstream from Hastinapura, has been a traditional enemy of Hastinapura, so this alliance is an opportunity for peace or for further war. To ensure peace while appeasing his son, Dhritarashtra divides the kingdom, giving the Pandavas the unliveable forest of *Kuru-jangala* ("the forest/jungle of the Kurus", also called *Khandavaprastha*[33]) to the west and south. The Pandavas create a glorious capital, *Indraprastha*[34], in the forest on the banks of the river Yamuna. They celebrate their success and show off their capital with a great feast. Duryodhana, still unhappy about the partition, is jealous of their success and plots to overthrow the Pandavas. He organizes a game of dice, a traditional pastime of the *kshatriya*[35] (the nobility), and invites an inexperienced Yudhishthira to play. Yudhishthira agrees, but when he comes to play, he finds himself facing an expert, *Shakuni*[36], playing for Duryodhana. In a high-stakes game Yudhishthira loses everything – that includes his brothers, then himself, and then finally his wife Draupadi.

The malice of the Kauravas is exposed when Draupadi, wagered without her consent, and lost, is dragged into the open court by her hair. Being a slave now, she is commanded to disrobe – a miracle prevents this assault and a briefly chastened Dhritarashtra nullifies the game. But Yudhishthira is persuaded to play a second dice game with a single throw for high stakes – the loser would go into exile in the forest for twelve years, followed by a year of being incognito – discovery would entail another twelve years of exile. Yudhishthira loses and the Pandavas go into exile with Draupadi.

The years in the forest are years of adventure and learning. The year of hiding also passes, again with adventures. After the thirteenth year, they ask for their kingdom back. The Kauravas refuse, setting the stage for the war. The war is a "Great War" –

---

[31] Phonetic: Pāncālə, Syllabic: Pa-nch-all-u(h)
[32] Phonetic: Drupədə, Syllabic: Dhrew-pu(s)-the
[33] Phonetic: Kʰāṇḍəvəprəstə, Syllabic: Khan-dove-a-prush-thu(d)
[34] Phonetic: Indrəprəstə, Syllabic: In-the-ru(n)-prush-thu(d)
[35] Phonetic: Kśətriyə, Syllabic: Shu(ck)-three-yu(p)
[36] Phonetic: Śəkunī, Syllabic: Shuck-oo(h)-knee

all the people of ancient India take part in it. The Kauravas field eleven armies, the Pandavas seven, for a total of almost two million warriors. The war, fought in *Kurukshetra*[37] ("the field of the Kurus") lasts eighteen days and almost all the warriors die.

Both sides commit atrocities in the war. For example, the Kauravas dishonourably mount a mass attack on the 15-year old *Abhimanyu*[38], son of Arjuna. The Pandavas lie to their old martial-arts teacher, *Drona*[39] (also called *Kutaja*[40]), who is fighting for the Kauravas, telling him that his son had been killed. Consequently, Drona abandons his weapons and leaves the battlefield. He is killed while unarmed, by Draupadi's brother (born to kill Drona in revenge for Drona's appropriation of Northern Panchala). Then, in the final duel of the war, Bhima violates the rules of one-on-one mace combat and attacks Duryodhana below the belt breaking his thighs. This act of cheating ends the war. Or so we would think. Even after the war is over and the fighting is ended, and while Duryodhana lies on the river-bank waiting for death, *Aswatthama*[41], the son of Drona, sets fire to the Pandava camp in the night and slaughters the Pandavas' children. The Pandavas inherit the kingdom even as the women of the world cry for their loss of loved ones.

A by-product of the war was the *Bhagavad-Gita*[42], sometimes considered a religious foundation for Hindu beliefs. On the verge of battle, Arjuna, the battle-chief of the Pandavas, has second thoughts about the legitimacy of killing the cousins, teachers, and friends who are arrayed against him alongside the Kauravas. His charioteer, Krishna, counsels him to adopt the attitude of *nishkāma-karma*[43] ("acting without attachment to the fruits of the action"). Krishna explains that at that point, war was inevitable, and it was Arjuna's duty and responsibility to fight for his side without attachment to the (also inevitable) resulting victory or defeat. His actions could not be dictated by the pleasant fantasy of winning or the horrors of losing or the pain that might follow, but be a response to the needs of the situation

---

[37] Phonetic: Kurukśétrə, Syllabic: Coup-rook-sha(pe)-thru(st)
[38] Phonetic: Əbʰimənyu, Syllabic: U(h)-beam-un-you
[39] Phonetic: Drōṇə, Syllabic: The-row-nu(h)
[40] Phonetic: Kuṭəjə, Syllabic: Coup-the-ja(r)
[41] Phonetic: Əśvəttāmə, Syllabic: (H)ush-vuth-a(h)-mu(h)
[42] Phonetic: Bʰəgəvəd-Gītə, Syllabic: Bug-gov-oth(er)-Gee(se)-thu(s)
[43] Phonetic: niś-kām-kərmə, Syllabic: niche-calm-cur-ma

– to the task to be accomplished, his role in performing the task, the morality or otherwise of the specific actions, and so on. The death of loved ones was a foregone conclusion and his unhappiness about that result could not be allowed to influence his immediate actions. Krishna reveals himself to be the incarnation of *Vishnu*[44], (the Preserver, and therefore qualified to make moral judgments); he also shows Arjuna his divine form as the Destroyer of Worlds (to assure Arjuna that the people who were to die were already dead and their death was not Arjuna's responsibility). This demonstration proves to be compelling, Arjuna's doubts vanish, and the war proceeds.

The story has an extended prologue and epilogue. The prologue is best described as Genesis – how the universe was created and the gods and demons came into existence, and how humans came to be. This cosmogony leads to a history of the first ancestors of the Kuru dynasty. The history of the dynasty reveals a familial theme of unusual royal succession, culminating in the birth of the cousins.

The epilogue covers the events that follow the war. This includes the lamentations of the survivors, an extended treatise on kingship and power, the establishment of suzerainty over the entire region of India, and finally, the death of the surviving Pandava allies (such as Krishna) and a fantastic story of the Pandavas' climb to heaven.

THE SELECTED EPISODES

These stories have been selected because they illustrate an aspect of *human* behaviour in response to a problem; and from the nature of the response, we can appreciate the condition of the world and of humanity in the past. I precede each story with a short commentary. I hope that this commentary is not a distraction arousing nit-picking debate while still providing a reasoned platform for debate., even if controversial.

MY APPROACH

As a scientist and atheist, I bring a sceptical attitude to religion and its attendant hagiography and mythology. At the same

---

[44] Phonetic: Viśnu, Syllabic: Wish-noo(n)

time, I enjoy stories of superheroes with unusual powers or weapons with unusual capabilities. The Mahabharata uses the actions of gods, the doctrine of karma, and the existence of magical beings to explain why certain acts and events were "just" and not happenstance. Unfortunately, this magical superstructure does not add much value to the story and detracts from it. An example of such detraction is the episode of the Crane-Demon's questions.

This story is titled *"Yakshaprasna[45]"* or "The Questions of the Yaksha". A yaksha is a mythical being from Indian mythology with magic powers, sometimes considered demonic. He (or she) can have many forms. In this story, he appears to be a crane. The yaksha may befriend an ordinary human, but is quick-to-anger and can be vengeful. The story is an adventure that is represented as exemplifying the wisdom of Yudhishthira – he answers the many questions asked by the yaksha. The story is much deeper than that – it exemplifies the principle that the powerful respect the rights of indigenous peoples; it is a tale of loyalty to the people who are in our power and of resolving conflicts in loyalty when trade-offs must be made. It is, most emphatically, not a simple story of one man's ability to answer puzzles.

Krishna, a character in the Mahabharata, is considered by many Indians to be an incarnation of the *supreme being[46]*, and many Indians will refer to him as "Lord Krishna", even when he acts in ways not expected of the One God. Many, but not all, variants of the Mahabharata do not refer to him in that way. Krishna performs a few miracles, for which secular explanations have been proposed. I cannot claim that the Mahabharata does NOT consider him to *be* god without stepping on sensitive toes. I deal with this by calling him "Krishna" rather than "Lord Krishna" and not including any of the miraculous stories in this selection.

I am not *against* magic – they can add an exciting element of fantasy to any story. The divine missiles called *astras* are a favourite fantasy weapon in Indian myth. These are fun, even if not realistic or scientific. I make use of them in a limited way.

---

[45] Phonetic: Yəkśəprəśnə, Syllabic: Yuck-shu(t)-pruss(ian)-nu(h)
[46] More commonly, capitalized as "Supreme Being".

One innovation that I have tried to adhere to was to call the participants by names that describe them positively. The Mahabharata is an extended lay of Victory – these were commissioned by the victors of a war. Such a lay, called a *Jaya*[47], would praise the heroes of the sponsoring side, and mock and denigrate the warriors on the losing side. This origin has coloured the epic.

Traditionally, both heroes and villains had many names. These variant names might describe a physical attribute or some behaviour (Bhima, one of the heroes, is called *Vrikodhara*[48], meaning "wolf-bellied" and "voracious eater" because of his eating habits); some identified by a parent ("Pandava" the children of Pandu) or earlier ancestor ("Kaurava" meaning descendant of Kuru); some identified by the city or land they came from ("Panchali" meaning Princess/Woman/Daughter of Panchala). Sometimes they were antonyms, possibly intended as a sardonic comment, or sometimes they were intended to mock the character, especially of villains. In the Mahabharata, the name of the leader of the losing side is traditionally given as *Duryodhana* ("stubborn, awkward fighter", but also maybe "tough fighter"), which is not considered a praiseworthy name. Occasionally, he is called *Suyodhana* [49]("good warrior") – by his friends and parents. We do not know if this was his *real* name, the name that may well have been his own. *I use Suyodhana exclusively instead of Duryodhana.*

This renaming experiment has not been a success with the readers of drafts of this collection. Both children and adults found this confusing. The ones who were already familiar with the Mahabharata were distracted by these names, as the traditional names are well known and my alternative names obscure. However, I feel this is a matter of principle and have continued to stick with it while being pragmatic about making sure readers would understood who was being referred to, by providing both names when needed.

---

[47] Phonetic: Jəyā, Syllabic: Ju(st)-ya

[48] Phonetic: Vrikōdərə, Syllabic: Vri-ko(h)-the-ru(h) – the first syllable does not occur in English.

[49] Phonetic: Suyōdənə, Syllabic: Sue-yo-the-nu(h)

The Education of the Princes

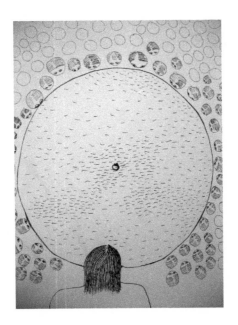

THE EDUCATION OF THE PRINCES

THE UNRULY GANG

When Pandu and Madri died, Kunti returned to Hastinapura from the forest with the five Pandava princes in tow. Devavrata Bhishma, their grand-uncle, and their uncle Dhritarashtra welcomed them, saddened by the news of Pandu's death. Dhritarashtra was older than Pandu, but being blind, he could not be the king; nonetheless, Pandu had treated him as his equal co-ruler. Abruptly, Pandu had exiled himself in the forest leaving the kingdom in the care of Bhishma and Dhritarashtra. Bhishma continued as Regent; Dhritarashtra had kept the title of King and Bhishma encouraged people to recognize Dhritarashtra as King. When the Pandavas came back, Dhritarashtra felt obliged to return Pandu's kindness and recognized Yudhishthira, who was sixteen years old, as the heir to the kingdom – it would be a few years before he could be crowned. Yudhishthira had a lot to learn as his training to be a King had been woefully lacking.

Kunti returns to Hastinapura

Dhritarashtra's own hundred sons, the Kauravas, were all younger so there was nobody to protest Yudhishthira's appointment as *heir apparent*.

Bhishma was the Regent. He administered the kingdom and was therefore too busy to educate the princes himself. The blind Dhritarashtra obviously could not. Since the hundred and four boys were still young, Bhishma placed them under the tutelage of his foster-brother Kripacharya, while he searched for an appropriate teacher. This had worked when the Pandavas were not there. But the arrival of the Pandavas created rivalry and tension.

The children became an unruly gang. They were restricted to a garden in which they could run wild and did. Kripacharya could not control the children. The Pandavas and the older Kauravas fought with each other and took up all his effort. He pleaded with them to be mindful of their dignity and their family's dignity and of the need to show respect to elders and teachers – these were not concepts the adolescent children were prepared to learn. Meanwhile the younger children ran around and nothing meaningful was learned. Classes in archery became one-on-one sessions with a selected child while the remaining hundred and four refused to sit and watch. The mace-fighting class could never get started because as soon as the maces were handed out, the war of words between the cousins became a clash of maces between Suyodhana and Bhima, while the others watched and cheered them on. By the early afternoon, Kripacharya would withdraw exhausted, leaving the children unsupervised.

Yudhishthira proclaimed himself King of the children's gang; Suyodhana resented this but could do nothing because of Bhima, Yudhishthira's brother and protector. Bhima was the biggest and the strongest of the children. He harassed and teased the Kauravas and they all hated him.

One day, Kripacharya had withdrawn in frustration and the children were left by themselves. Some of them were playing with a ball. A scuffle over picking up the ball became a fight. There was no referee. Yudhishthira and Bhima were not playing – Bhima fetched the ball, handed it to Yudhishthira, and asked him to be the judge to decide who should get it. Yudhishthira gave it to Nakula. The Kauravas protested and Suyodhana, also not playing, questioned Yudhishthira's right to be the referee. Yudhishthira was nettled – he took out Pandu's ring which he carried around and displayed it – as the holder of the King's ring, he asserted his right be their leader, judge, and referee. Suyodhana grabbed at his hand, Yudhishthira pulled back, the ball flew out of his hand and so did the ring. Both objects went flying into a well.

The children screamed. Bhima ran to the well and looked down. The others followed and crowded around the well – all hundred and four could not fit around the rim, but they tried. The rim had been built up with brick to about a little more than one hand -- it was a miracle that nobody fell in. Bhima and the older children leaned over and looked in. The sides of the well had handholds and footholds that an expert climber could have used, but not the children who had been warned not to climb into it. And the prospect was daunting and even Bhima did not want to climb down. The ball could be seen floating in the water about twenty feet below. The water was not deep, barely two or three hands, and at the right angle, they could see the glint of the ring at the bottom. The older boys debated and came up with the idea of creating an upside-down human chain dangling into the well. Volunteers were needed, but nobody would volunteer. Nobody wanted to go into the well – that might be too dangerous and get the volunteer into trouble even if they survived.

They would have to ask an adult for help. That would require explaining how this accident happened and who was responsible. Nobody wanted that. Yudhishthira and Suyodhana were senior-most and they were left blaming each other for the loss of the ring and the ball.

Gradually the children quieted down. They huddled to come up with a story that would avoid any punishments. That was when they noticed the visitor. Kripa had a visitor – his sister's husband. He was of medium height, but despite being a Brahmin, he was well-built and had the bulging pectoral and upper arm muscles of an archer. He had come earlier when Kripacharya had been teaching them and spoken quietly with their teacher and then wandered off into the garden. He made no noise when he moved and nobody had noticed him coming and watching them. He was smiling. It seemed that he knew something they did not. He was also the only adult around, and he was new and was unlikely to ask uncomfortable questions, so Yudhishthira approached him and asked for help.

Kutaja, for that was his name, laughed when they described the problem. He said, "I am merely a Brahmin. You are all powerful Kshatriyas. Why can't you do it yourself?"

Yudhishthira said, "We are only children. Please, sir, help us." Kutaja considered his request and said, "What can I do?". One of the children shouted, "Maybe you have some Brahmin magic?" All the others nodded their heads and repeated what he said – the need for magic seemed obvious. The demand for magic buzzed through the collected children and returned as a chorus.

A Mystic Sign

The children said, "Brahmin magic! Show us some Brahmin magic."

Bhima was particularly loud. He gestured to the others with

his arms and their voices rose. He said, "Yeah! Yeah! Magic!" and the crowd took up the slogan, chanting it in unison. The children pretended to carve out mysterious symbols in the air and mouthed the mystic sound "OM!" In this manner, they added their pleas to Yudhishthira's request.

Kutaja stood up. Yudhishthira could not interpret his face. *Was he upset? Did he think it was too forward to have made such a request?*

Kutaja did not know whether to laugh or to be angry. Bhima seemed to be teasing him.

Kutaja said, "I know some Kshatriya magic as well. Let me show you your kind instead."

He walked over to the well and looked in. "Hah! This is easy. Are you sure, Prince Bhima, that you don't want to do this by yourself without magic? I can tie a rope to you and throw you in."

Bhima said, "No, no, no. I think that would be too hard." He wondered if this strange man was serious.

Suyodhana saw that Bhima was nervous. He chanted, "Scaredy-cat! You are a scaredy-cat."

Bhima blinked his eyes rapidly and his mouth formed a crooked smile. His eyes became small – the other Kauravas saw the tension in his face and took up the chant, "Scaredy-Cat! Scaredy-Cat!"

Bhima said to Suyodhana, "I am the biggest among all of us. Why don't we pick somebody smaller than a bucket and send him down the well? How about your smallest brother?"

Bhima looked around and ran to Vikarna who was about five years old and very small. He picked him up, rushed back to the well, when he stopped as though he had run into a wall. Kutaja did not seem to be exerting himself at all, but his hand on Bhima's shoulder had brought Bhima's rush to a stop. Meanwhile the Kauravas shouted for him to stop and Vikarna began to scream.

Kutaja's voice hardened. "Put him down, child! I will be your *drona*[50] and recover your ball." Bhima heard the voice and let Vikarna go.

Kutaja's Magic

The children were awed. They crowded around the small well in a bunch several children deep and only the first two rows could see what the man was doing. They asked many questions. "What's going on?"; "Who's the man"; "Will he go into the well?", and demands – "Lemme see! Lemme see!". The resulting buzz made them sound like a beehive full of angry bees.

Kutaja looked around the well. From one side of the well, a trough led to the edge of a field that bordered the children's garden. An irrigation channel laid with brick ran around the perimeter of the field. Clumps of elephant grass grew tall at irregular intervals along the outer edge of the irrigation channel. He went over to the nearest clump, grabbed a handful of stalks, and with a jerk pulled them out. He brought them back to the well. He stripped one stalk of its leaves. Then with a fingernail he sliced one end and made it sharp. He angled it down into the well and moved his hands. He muttered something under his breath.

Arjuna was fascinated. *He is making an astra!* he thought. *What god was he invoking?* Arjuna had always been excited by the idea of *astras*, the magical missiles that invoked a god's power. And here was somebody who knew them -- he could teach them, whenever he visited.

An *astra* is made

The other boys crowded around the well, struggling to see what was happening. A hundred and four kids crowded around a small well, all looking intently at one man. They pushed, yelled, and elbowed each other. Kutaja raised his finger to his lips, "Silence," he said. In an instant, the unruly mob was quiet. Yudhishthira was amazed at the power of Kutaja's voice. The idea struck him: *This is no mere Brahmin visitor. He could teach me how to command an army, rule a kingdom.*

---

[50] Phonetic: Drōnə; Syllabic: drone-u(h); refers to a wooden jar, sometimes called a "bucket" used as part of a Vedic ritual.

Kutaja let the blade of grass drop and as the boys watched it fell straight and embedded itself in the ball.   A sound "aaaahhhh" swept the through the multitude.

Kutaja then repeated this procedure, except this time – it was amazing to see – the blade of grass embedded itself in the end of the previous one. The boys watched in silence and in awe. "This is no mere Brahmin" marvelled Arjuna, "I want him to teach me archery and astras, so I can be the best archer in the Universe."

Each stalk was about two three feet long. Five more times Kutaja sent a blade and a long chain of grass extended almost to the top of the well, but well within the range of Kutaja's hands. Kutaja reached over and grabbed the end of the last blade and slowly, very slowly, pulled on it, muttering all the while. Slowly, very slowly, the entire assembly with the ball at the end came away from the water. Kutaja kept pulling on the blades until the ball was near his hand and then he caught it. He stopped the muttering and as soon as he did, the blades became unstuck and fell to the ground, but Kutaja had the ball.

The princes leaped and hollered with joy. This is no mere Brahmin, thought Suyodhana. I want him to teach me his magic, so that I can accomplish great things.

The other boys shouted, "Wonderful! Amazing!" The smaller children who had been further back were still asking questions:

"Who's the man?"

"How did he do it?"

There was no answer and the children muttered and fought and shouted to be at the front of a circle that formed around the man. Yudhishthira waved for silence, but the children continued shouting. Kutaja raised his hand.

Everybody fell silent. "Sir!" Yudhishthira said, very formally, "Would you be able to fetch my ring that has fallen in as well."

Kutaja looked at him. "Do you have a bow?" he asked. "I do!" said Arjuna, and handed him his children's bow. Kutaja took the bow and smiled at the wide-open look in Arjuna's eyes. He said, "May you always be prepared with a bow, young prince."

A bow for Kutaja

Kutaja took an arrow and tied a string to it. He

then took the bow and notched the arrow and aimed it into the well and let it go. The arrow went straight into the ring and the impact made the ring bounce and when it landed it was askew on the arrowhead. Kutaja pulled on the string and brought up the arrow and the ring!

"Sir!" said Yudhishthira as he accepted the ring, "You are not a mere visitor here. Who are you?"

Kutaja said to Yudhishthira, "Tell your grandsire that the Bucket is here."

"The Bucket?" Yudhishthira echoed. *Did he mean that?*

"Yes, *Kutaja*, the bucket," repeated Kutaja.

That was interesting, Yudhishthira thought.

Somebody said, "He said he was a bucket." "A bucket?", "Yeah!" "Strange." Kutaja raised his hand and the children all fell quiet and stopped moving.

Yudhishthira looked at Bhima. Bhima left to fetch Bhishma. Everybody else watched Kutaja in case he did something interesting. Everybody was quiet. A short time later, there was some activity at the gate to the playground. Some soldiers entered and formed a guard. Bhishma came in, striding quickly, Bhima running beside him. He came directly to the children and they parted to let him in.

"What's going on here?" said Bhishma addressing the outermost ring of boys and looking intently at one of the Kauravas.

The boy was awed by his granduncles' presence. "I don't know sir. He called himself the Bucket?"

Kutaja and Yudhishthira turned when they heard Bhishma's voice. Yudhishthira giggled when he heard the answer and glanced at Kutaja to see if he was offended. He was relieved – Kutaja was smiling.

When Bhishma first saw Kutaja   the children were surrounding him and they seemed to be under his control. Bhishma came up to Yudhishthira and Kutaja and said to the man, "Who are you? How did you get so deep into the palace grounds?"

Yudhishthira said, "Sir! He has been most helpful. He calls

himself Kutaja."

Bhishma realized who the man was. His foster-sister Kripi had come for a visit some months ago and her husband was expected.

Bhishma said, "Kutaja! You are Kripi's husband. You are most welcome. I have been looking forward to your visit! You have ignored far too many of my messages. No matter! I am glad you are here. I hope the children have not been the cause of any trouble. When Kripi came back, I expected that you would follow soon after. We have been waiting weeks for you."

"Great one!" said Kutaja, "Thank you for your welcome. I was obliged to go to Panchala and meet Drupada first. Now any debt may owe him has been settled. I am free of that obligation. I am only sorry I could only come at this time."

Bhishma said, "I was going to invite you to stay and teach the children."

"I assume these are the children. I will gladly teach them."

"Wonderful. I will meet with you later today – for now can you take them on as your pupils!"

Thus, Kutaja became the teacher of the Pandavas and the Kauravas.

The Test

Kutaja taught the children a variety of martial arts – riding and controlling horses, fighting from chariots, sword fighting and fencing, mace fighting, archery, wrestling, and fighting without weapons. Kutaja was a hard teacher. He would reprimand anyone who watched another student during practice – "Face yourself" was his favourite expression. Occasionally he would stand in front of a student practicing a fencing pattern, look them steadily in the eye and stay just out of range of the sword. This was disconcerting and they did not know what to do. At the archery range he would come up to one of them as they were aiming for the target and stand beside them. When they released the arrow his hands would snap and snatch the arrow in mid-air leaving the bow. Then he would tell them to return to the first exercise which consisted of firing an imaginary arrow with a bow. It was a relief, sometimes, to return to something physically hard like running in and around the forest for an hour. After a year of training, Kutaja informed the children that he would test them in what they had learned.

They had all gained in strength that year, but Bhima was still the strongest and he was sure he would win any match of strength. Suyodhana thought he could defeat Bhima in mace-fighting because he had learned tricks by watching the street-corner performers who performed mace fights for entertainment. These were unorthodox techniques that Kutaja had not taught them.

Bhima's mace

Arjuna hoped that archery would be one of the tests. Yudhishthira was disgusted – he felt that he had learned nothing that year and he was the oldest. Kutaja had taught nothing about commanding an army! Nakula felt he had learned only a little about his favourite fighting skill – fighting from a horse. He loved the feeling of height that riding a horse provided him and he knew that he struck a handsome figure when seated on a horse. Sahadeva knew of Kutaja's reputation as a spymaster but despite all the hints that Sahadeva had dropped, Kutaja had not taught them the tricks of a professional spy. Duhshasana, the second oldest Kaurava, was bored with the interminable exercises.

The children had never been tested before. They looked at each other then looked at Yudhishthira and Suyodhana. Suyodhana said, "Why?" as the same time as Yudhishthira said, "What kind of test?"

"Wait and see," said their teacher. The next day they came to the practice ground and found it transformed. The ground had been cleared of all the practice paraphernalia – archery targets, sand pits for wrestling, bundles of hay for sword practice – all gone. The ground was empty except for a tall tower in the middle and next to it a small circle was drawn on the ground. Seated some distance from the tower were Bhishma and Kripacharya. Kutaja stood nearby in his alert pose. The boys lined up in front of Kutaja, all one hundred and five of them, the youngest in front and the oldest in the back and at a gesture, they sat down.

Kutaja pointed to the top of the tower. His voice, quiet but clear, reached the Pandavas who were sitting together in the back. "There is a target up there. It is a bird of straw with a jewel for an eye. The test is your ability to shoot an arrow and hit the eye. Yudhishthira, please step into the centre."

The Target   An uncertain Yudhishthira picked up his bow and an arrow, walked slowly across the rows of his cousins and stepped into the circle. *Something is wrong,* he thought. He raised the bow and notched the arrow. Kutaja frowned. "You may go back," he said. Confused, Yudhishthira stepped back. Suyodhana and Duhshasana exchanged looks. Duhshasana giggled. He stopped when Kutaja faced to look at him.

"Bhima," called Kutaja.

Bhima was frowning, his brow had hooded over his eyes. *Why had Yudhishthira failed?* Bhima thought. *He did not even get to fire!* He picked up his bow and arrow and stepped into the circle. He waited for a command from Kutaja. "What do you see?" asked Kutaja. Bhima was relieved – that's what Yudhishthira had done wrong. He looked up at the target. He could see the bird and the jewel glittered in the morning sun. *He is testing the clarity of my vision. I should be as accurate and complete as I can be.*

Bhima said, "The bird of straw is perched on the top ledge. It is tied to a post with rope. The eye gleams in the sun. The ..."

Kutaja raised a hand, "You may go now. Next. Suyodhana."

Bhima stepped out. The frown had returned. *What had happened?*

Suyodhana coughed to stifle his laugh. He looked away so that Kutaja would not see his smirk. Then he realized that Kutaja had called his name. He picked up his bow and arrow. As he passed by a dejected Bhima returning to his place, he poked him with his bow. Bhima glared at him but Suyodhana kept going.

It's obvious what they did wrong. Lucky for me, I wasn't the first. Otherwise I'd look like those two fools. He stepped into the ring and waited for Kutaja's question.

"What do you see?"

"I see a bird."

"What else do you see?"

Suyodhana paused. *What did he mean by that? Darn! There were more questions in the test. Why did he not call Arjuna next?* Suyodhana's mind raced with ideas – Kutaja frequently mentioned the requirement that a warrior had to be aware of all that was relevant. *Bhima failed because he described irrelevant attributes of the bird.* If this was a battle, one would be surrounded by both enemies and friends. *He needed to be aware of potential enemies. Who were the enemies here? The other birds on the roof? His cousins? Anybody?* He hesitated as long as he dared and decided on an answer.

"I see my cousins. I see the boundary of the circle. I see ..."

Kutaja said, "Stop. You may go." Chagrined, Suyodhana stepped out and glared at Duhshasana in case he was thinking of giggling. It would be Arjuna's turn to be humiliated next.

That was not what happened. Kutaja skipped Arjuna. One after the other, he called all the others who were old enough to fire an arrow, disqualifying them one by one. Finally, it was Arjuna's turn. He was the last one.

"What do you see?"

"I see a jewel, shining," said Arjuna.

"What else do you see?"

The TARGET

"Nothing else,"

"Get ready to shoot," commanded Kutaja. Arjuna notched an arrow and pulled the bow-string past his ear. Then he waited.

Kutaja said, "What do you see now?"

"A jewel, shining."

"Release!" said Kutaja

Arjuna let go of the bow-string and the arrow flew and went through the eye of the bird. The jewel fell to the ground. The children watching erupted with excitement – after all those failures, somebody has succeeded. The Pandavas ran to Arjuna to congratulate him. Bhima's hug enveloped his brother so joyfully that Arjuna disappeared from view.

Suyodhana and Duhshasana grimaced. Their brothers looked to them for guidance. Suyodhana thought, *I must save face for all of us, How?* After hesitating for less than a vighati[51], Suyodhana said, "So we would have been allowed to shoot an arrow at the bird, if we had been blind like Arjuna?"

Kutaja looked at Suyodhana, "Is that what you think happened?"

Suyodhana spoke very quietly so that only Kutaja and Duhshasana heard. He said, "No. As usual, you are partial to him."

Kutaja said, "Arjuna will be the best archer in the world. You, dear prince, can grumble about that or choose to be the best at what you can do. If I can, I will make that happen. It is for you to choose."

Suyodhana's eyes narrowed and he said, "I want to be the best with the mace."

At that Bhima turned and heard Kutaja say, "So be it – you shall be the best mace-fighter in the world." Bhima's ears reddened. *I wanted to be the best mace-fighter.* He stepped in front of Kutaja and said, "I want to be the best wrestler."

"So be it," said Kutaja.

"I want to be the best commander on the field," said Yudhishthira.

"So be it," said Kutaja.

That released the floodgates of desire and the pupils' jostled each other coming up to their teacher with their wishes. However, Kutaja was done for that day and no more promises were made.

---

[51]The day from dawn to dusk was divided into 60 *ghaṭis,* and each ghati was 60 *vighaṭis,* A vighati is 24 seconds; a ghati is 24 minutes.

A King's Friend

A KING'S FRIEND

THE INSULT

"Can't you stop the baby from crying?" Kutaja said to his wife *Kripi*[52]. "I cannot hear myself think."

Kripi said, "How can I do that? I have not eaten for a day and my breasts have little milk. We have no cows or goats to give us milk. You missed going to the feast this morning, because you were too engrossed in your thinking to go early. You went late, and of course, you did not bring home anything. Where is the baby going to get its food? Will it devour my liver? What do you think – I can make food appear like a miracle?"

"Don't mind me," said Kutaja, "I can get by without eating."

Kripi stopped pushing the baby swing and faced her husband. "What do you think I am talking about? *I* can get by without eating. Your hunger is not my concern right now. Even if I were hungry, I would not be concerned. I am concerned about your child. I am concerned about your child

Empty Pots

here who is starving because his mother has no food because his father, her husband, thinks that he has no role to play in bringing food to the house because he must spend his time becoming a more perfect warrior and a more perfect strategist. You went with all the other brahmins to visit *Parashurama*[53] – they came back within a month carrying wealth to last a year; you came back six months later with nothing? Did you forget me during that time? If it weren't for the other women in this settlement, I would have died before giving birth to this god-forsaken boy you so cherish. You can't even feed him, let alone clothe and shelter him! Do something about this, now," she said. She lifted the child out of the swing and brought him to his father. "Here," she said, "Feed him, if you can." She went into a corner of the cottage and lay down on the ground and turned her face to the wall.

---

[52] Phonetic: Kripi; Syllabic: Cri-pee.
[53] Phonetic: Pərəśurāmə; Syllabic: Per-u(h)-shoe-a(h)-mu(h).

The Ancient Hero

Kutaja looked down at his squalling son and sighed. He was the only brahmin from the settlement who had received nothing material from Parashurama the *Bhargava*[54]. The journey to Parashurama's Himalayan abode had been difficult and the thin air of the hills had made Kutaja sick. He had fallen behind the others and arrived a day late to find that all of Parashurama's wealth had been distributed. One of his neighbours had even received Parashurama's own massive iron plough that doubled as his weapon of choice. Parashurama's had nothing to give Kutaja, but he did not want to send him away with nothing. The great sage and warrior had offered him the gift of training with him for six months as a consolation. Kutaja had eagerly accepted, for Parashurama was legendary for his knowledge of magic weapons. He, Kutaja, had not even bothered to check with his pregnant wife but had sent a messenger. Six months later, he had come back home empty-handed to face a crisis.

His mouth would lock into a smile, whenever he gazed at his son. *If only the child's existence had not made my own life so difficult, I would be the happiest man in this world.* When he first saw Kripi, he knew he wanted to marry her. Kripi and her twin brother *Kripa* [55]were the foster children of Shantanu, the King of Hastinapura. She had accompanied her foster-father Shantanu, his son Devavrata, and her brother Kripa. Kutaja and Kripi were drawn to each other and it showed. At sixteen, Kripi was considered marriageable, so they were married. Kutaja envisioned the course of their life as straight and simple. That was not how it worked out. Complexities began from the beginning, almost but not quite, from the first wedded day.

Kutaja's father *Bharadvaja*[56] was one of the foremost teachers of the martial arts and of royal strategy. His ashram housed the many students who came to him and their *guru-dakshina*[57] was what provided for the entire academy. The academy was famous – Bharadvaja, it's teachers, and, even his young son Kutaja,

---

[54] Phonetic: Bʰārgəvə; Syllabic: Bar-gov-u(h)
[55] This is an abbreviated form of Kripācāryə. Phonetic: Kripā; Syllabic: Cri-pa.
[56] Phonetic: Bʰərədvājə, Syllabic: Bu(s)-ru(b)-the-va(st)-ju(h)
[57] The traditional gift to a Guru at the end of training. Phonetic: Goo(d)-roo(d)-the-(l)uck-sheen-u(h).

received invitations to visit kingdoms and advise the king, the king's counsellors, or to train the military. Often, Bharadvaja would ask Kutaja to stay behind and supervise their continued training until they achieved mastery. As a result, Kutaja was away much of the time. Kutaja and Kripi remained childless for a long time[58]. Aswatthama was a child they had been waiting for.

The intervening years had not been good for the academy – there were no military confrontations and people focused on escaping the effects of the drying Sarasvati. Attendance at the academy started falling after Bharadvaja's withdrawal and then death. Kutaja could not stop the decline and had finally closed the academy and they had moved to a nearby village where Kripi would have help taking care of the baby when Kutaja was away.

While Kutaja contemplated the child, Kripi got up and came over. "Give him back to me," she said. "I will get some fresh cow's milk from Shashikala next door." She took the baby and placed him in a basket lined with cloth.

Kutaja said, "I have an idea. I will visit my old friend Drupada."

A sound came from the corner. Kripi glared up at him, her face purple and eyes narrowed. "Your old friend Drupada," she said, an echo.

"Every time we discuss our life, you bring up this imaginary friend. Drupada, King of Panchala, you say, "I will ask him for help." After saying that you do nothing and I find some other way to resolve the problem, while you go on your way thinking great thoughts. When your father died, you said, *I will visit my old friend Drupada*. It did not happen – we stayed until you closed your father's school. At the last minute, I found us this cottage to live in and Drupada was forgotten once more."

Kripi

"It was wrong," said Kutaja, "I should have asked Drupada for help the very first time."

"My dear husband," Kripi responded, "There is much you

---

[58] One estimate (to be taken with a pinch of salt) that may be derived from the timeline of the Mahabharata, was that Aswatthama was born when Kutaja was in his eighties and Kripi was only a bit younger, possibly seventy-nine or so.

should have done. That is in the past. What do I do now? We have run out of everything. Let me go to my brother's house. You can pay the long-postponed visit to Drupada. Come back with honours. In the meantime, at least my brother will not let my son and I starve."

She said that and there was no changing her mind – nothing he said could persuade her and she left the same day for Hastinapura where her twin brother, Kripa was now the teacher and advisor to the ruling family.

A VISIT TO PANCHALA

Having seen off Kripi and Aswatthama, Kutaja set off for Panchala. It was downstream and not a long trip by boat, but the return would be upstream and expensive. Kutaja had with him a finely woven cotton shawl from the Sindhu country, a small collection of incense sticks, and his most valuable possession, some cherry-sized balls of sandalwood. As a brahmin he offered to bless the boats he was ferried on. Once, the boatman laughed and refused to take any payment; more often, the owner scowled and refused. Since the trip to *Kampilya*[59] was mostly downstream he only gave up some of the sandalwood. Occasionally he found somebody willing to take him in exchange for a ritual blessing. In this way, he made his way to Drupada's kingdom. By the time he reached the capital, he was hungry and had almost nothing of his own.

It was late in the afternoon but he made his way directly to his friend's palace. The guards stopped him. He was dishevelled from his travels and they looked dubious when he announced that he had come to see the king. "The morning session of the court is over," they told him, but Kutaja was not deterred. "I am not a petitioner," he said, "Just let the king know that his friend, the Bucket, is here."

The guards conferred with each other, occasionally glancing at him. One of them came back to him with a stoic look in his face, as though suffering from dyspepsia. "The bucket? You are

---

[59] Phonetic: Kāmpilyə; Syllabic: Calm-pill-yu(h).

sure?" he asked. Kutaja was irritated. The guards' attitude bothered him. He felt that they should be more deferential to a brahmin visitor. His stomach rumbled to remind him that he had not eaten and he rebuked the guards, "Yes, didn't you hear me? Tell him that his friend the bucket is here. Be quick about it, my man. He will not be happy if you are tardy."

Drupada had ended the court session early that day and was in his garden with his wife. The inner guards of the palace had been instructed that he was not to be disturbed. The message made its way to the officer of the chambers. He sent back a message that the petitioner should come back the next day as the king was not to be disturbed.

Kutaja had hoped and half-expected that his old friend, the king, would come as soon as he heard that his friend Kutaja was at the gate. The guards were apparently too fearful to pass on his message. They were well-trained, disciplined, and obeyed orders, the sign of a well-managed security force. However, he was determined that he would stay at the gates of the palace. The guards were determined that he should not stay at the palace gates and demanded that he leave. That did not sit well with Kutaja – he was a proud man; he was not just any brahmin, but a guru to warriors and a man of honour. He refused to leave. The guards sent for the police who tried to arrest Kutaja. Kutaja would have resisted, but then he realized that creating a ruckus at the entrance to his friend's palace was not dignified. He acquiesced to the police request and left.

For three days he awaited the summons of the king. Finally he concluded that the king had not received his message and he went for the morning audience.

The King

His turn came and he announced himself. He was gratified by Drupada's response, for the king came down and escorted him publicly to a seat of honour. It was tedious, for he had to sit through the king's public audience all morning. When the event was over, the king rose and had apparently forgotten that Kutaja was present and the procession began to leave. Kutaja stood up and exclaimed, "Drupada, my friend!"

The king turned and looked at him with a frown on his brow. "Oh, brahmin," he said, "You address me as 'friend'?"

"Don't you recognize me? I am Kutaja, the son of Bharadvaja. We knew each other as children."

"I recognized you as the learned scholar and honoured you as befits one. What more did you want?"

Kutaja's heart raced. He felt a sour taste in his mouth and his stomach churned as he comprehended these words. His next words surprised even him, "We called each other friend, when we were students in my father's ashram! Are we not friends still?"

"You did not ask for anything, but even so, I have fed you from my table with the other noble ones and great warriors who swear allegiance to me. How can a pauper like you be a friend to a rich and powerful ruler like me?"

Kutaja hesitated, his emotions too visible on his face. He said, "When we were children you vowed that we would be friends forever."

Drupada's brow wrinkled and his eyes narrowed. Then he said, "When we were children, I was as much of a pauper as you. I was not yet my father's heir-apparent, just another of his children. Friendship between you and me was possible then."

Kutaja said, "You said that if you ever came to rule Panchala-desha, you would even share your kingdom with me as an equal!"

Drupada said, "In the emotion of that time, I may have said things. Do not bring them up again.

You expect to share my kingdom? What army do you bring that would either help me or overcome me? Or have you become so addled in your dotage that you seek to hold me to a childhood game?"

Drupada turned his back and started to leave the room. At the edge of the doorway, he turned and said, "You asked for nothing in public, so I acknowledged and honoured you with a seat next to me. If you wish a gift from me, ask for it at tomorrow's audience. Good day."

Kutaja fell silent. This rejection of his claim to a childhood friendship was an arrow to the core of his self; the too-public display of contempt filled his mouth with ashes; his brain whirled as all the alternatives he had hoped for crumbled to dust. He thought of his wife and child waiting in Hastinapura and his sorrow changed to anger. "Beware, O King!" he said.

Drupada's tone changed from scorn to anger and his face was bright red. "You dare to warn me, you penniless scoundrel! Guards! Arrest this brahmin!"

Drupada turned to his chief minister, "Teach this braggart a lesson."

Saying that, he left with his entourage. The guards moved towards Kutaja, tied his hands with rope and took him to an underground dungeon.

A Lesson

Kutaja spent three days in jail as a common prisoner and then was taken to the ferry on the banks of the Ganga and released with instructions to never return. The ferry crossed over the Ganga and then went upstream hugging the banks and stopping whenever a market was visible.

Thus Kutaja crossed the Ganga and entered the Hastinapura side. At the ferry, he mentioned his brother-in-law Kripa's name. Instantly, the administrator of the ferry arranged for Kutaja to be escorted to the capital. There, Kutaja was welcomed by his father-in-law and by his wife. Kutaja refused to talk about his journey – it had taken almost three months and he had come back empty-handed. Kripi did not push him. He held Aswatthama in his arms for a long time, and when he put him down, the boy insisted on showing him the house they were living in, the neighbourhood and his playmates. Holding the boy gave him some peace from the hurt that smouldered in his heart.

Failure

THE OFFERING TO THE GURU

Shortly after his arrival, Kutaja became teacher to the Pandavas and Kauravas. It took some time for them to get comfortable with him. When he had been accepted as their teacher and he trusted their discretion, he called them in for a meeting. Kutaja said, "I have a task buried deep in my heart that I wish to see done. It will be your *guru-dakshina,* your offering to the teacher and your payment for your education. Promise me that when you have mastered your weapons, you will perform this task for me."

Suyodhana looked at his brothers and they looked to him. His brow furrowed and his eyes narrowed. *Why are we being asked to do this for this servant?* he thought.

"Are you not paid by Bhishma and maintained by my father's kingdom?" Suyodhana said, "Why do we owe you guru-dakshina? In any case, isn't guru-dakshina paid only if we stay with you in your ashram? You are housed by us."

Yudhishthira pondered and began to formulate an answer, "Sire, we can…" but he was interrupted by Arjuna who said, "Of course, guru-ji, we will do this for you". He turned to his brothers with challenge in his eyes, but he need not have worried, for Bhima, Nakula, and Sahadeva were nodding their heads in assent and all Yudhishthira could add was, "… but will the elders of Hastinapura approve?"

Kutaja shrugged and said, "They will not care as long as you are safe." He embraced Arjuna fondly.

Suyodhana felt he had done something wrong. He said, "Guru-ji, if father and grand-uncle will not object, we will certainly do it."

Five years passed. Arjuna, Kutaja's favourite, had become an accomplished archer. His ability to shoot from a chariot being driven at full tilt awed everybody. Bhima was a champion wrestler; Suyodhana was an accomplished mace-wielder. Yudhishthira was deemed to be calm, even-tempered and wise.

One older man had joined the group at Suyodhana's insistence – Karna, the charioteer's son, who considered himself Arjuna's enemy and Suyodhana's friend, had been accepted as Kutaja's pupil.

Kutaja called Karna, Yudhishthira, Suyodhana, Bhima, Arjuna, and Duhshasana to a meeting. "You are not children anymore," he said. The students bowed in acknowledgement. He continued, "It is time for you to render unto me your payment, guru-dakshina, in exchange for my teaching."

"Please command us, and we will do your bidding," chorused the six pupils. "In these five years, you have taught us much. Is there some treasure you would like us to fetch? Is there some deed you wish us to accomplish using these skills that came to us through you?"

"Do you remember my request five years ago?" said Kutaja. All but Karna did. The Kauravas also recalled that they had not been willing to pledge unconditionally. "I bear a grudge against Drupada the king of Panchala and I wish to teach him a lesson. You will join me in a raid to capture him."

"All of you need not come," said Kutaja to Suyodhana and Duhshasana, "Arjuna will do. Anybody else wishes to drop out, they can."

Suyodhana and Karna were incensed. This was their first opportunity for a real battle and they were to be deprived of it because of some childhood qualms. Karna interrupted, "The Kauravas and I will bring Drupada to you immediately." With that Karna and Suyodhana organized a raiding party and rushed off. They came back the next day, their heads hanging in shame for they had crossed at the ferry and the soldiers at the other end had raised an alarm. The small size of the raiding party and their loud boasts had made them an easy target. Drupada had not even come himself and had sent a small force that had easily overwhelmed them. The Kauravas managed to get back across the river leaving behind most of their men.

Kutaja said, "Arjuna is all I need to accomplish this."

Yudhishthira said, "Let us come along to help Arjuna."

"Then you must obey me implicitly. Prepare for a battle," said Kutaja. "Follow me and obey all my directions."

Kutaja and the Pandavas went by themselves to the north.

Kutaja arranged for news to be delivered to Drupada that Hastinapura was planning a major raid of Ahicchatra in the north and that a smaller raiding party would attack Kampilya the capital. Karna and Suyodhana's unexpected sortie into Panchala seemed to confirm the possibility of an attack as well as the possibility that Ahicchatra was the real target. As Kutaja expected, Drupada left a small force to defend Kampilya and headed to Ahicchatra himself to defend the northern city.

When Drupada had left, and was gone a few days, the band set out from the city of Hastinapura across the Ganga and approached Kampilya. At the same time news was sent to Drupada that Kampilya had been attacked by a large force. Fearing a disaster, Drupada headed back south with a small fast force as the vanguard of the larger, slower army. This was

Kutaja's plan – Drupada's small band was ambushed by Arjuna and the Pandavas. In the melee, Drupada was isolated, and many of his men killed and some captured. Arjuna challenged Drupada to a duel, defeated him, and bound him. Some of Drupada's closest ministers were also captured. The Pandavas blindfolded them and the team crossed the Ganga and went north on the Hastinapura side, until they reached the crossing to Ahicchatra where a Hastinapura force was facing the Panchala force.

Drupada was brought blindfolded before Kutaja. "Who are you?" questioned Kutaja, "How should I treat you?"

Captured   "I am Drupada, son of Prsata," said Drupada, and gave the traditional answer to the challenge, "and I should be treated like a King.[60]"

"A conqueror is not the equal of the conquered," said Kutaja, "The one who conquers is the true king. How can I treat one who is not a king like a king? Can a slave be the equal of a ruler? Can a beggar, even a royal beggar, be the equal of a victor? How can one who is not a king be a friend to one who is a king?"

Drupada recognized the charge and hung his head. "Kutaja, my friend," he began, but Kutaja was in no mood to listen.

Kutaja said, "You are my prisoner, and your kingdom is forfeit to me. Do you acknowledge that?"

"Yes."

"I shall retain Panchala north of the Ganga and the city of Ahicchatra as my fiefdom. I give you back, as a gift, the south and the great city of Kampilya."

"Thank you. You are most generous," said Drupada, swallowing his pride.

Kutaja ordered the blindfolds taken off Drupada and his ministers.

---

[60] This can be recognized as the response that Porus is supposed to have made when the Greek conqueror Alexander captured him. It is often presented as an indication of Porus's pride, that was not diminished even after being captured. The truth is probably a bit more complex – I think that this statement says, "Either deal with me as your equal, or kill me and rule my kingdom – there is no middle path."

"We are now equals, are we not?" asked Kutaja.

"Yes."

"Once more, o King, I seek your friendship. You know that a king can only be a friend to another king. We are both kings now. We can both occupy a high place and we can be friends, again."

Drupada looked down and away, his shoulders slumped. *I will not beg!*

"I was wrong to be so arrogant. Forgive me. Let us be friends as only kings can be friends.[61]"

He then turned to the Pandavas standing silently by.

"Who are these young warriors who overcame me?"

Drupada's thoughts were like a wild-fire scorching him internally. *I have nothing against them. Its Kutaja I want revenge on. I will get my revenge. Just as Kutaja used these boys to be revenged on me, I will use these boys. I will get my revenge. I will turn them against Kutaja.*

Kutaja smiled broadly as he looked at his boys. "These are my best students, the Pandavas." answered Kutaja, his pride surfacing, "Arjuna, the master of archery and the chariot, defeated you. Bhima of the powerful arms, bound you and your ministers. Yudhishthira, the eldest, planned the ambush."

"They are formidable warriors," said Drupada, "Hastinapura is fortunate in having them as its future rulers."

In this manner, Kutaja acquired a fiefdom. He continued to be the teacher for the Pandavas and the Kauravas, and acknowledged the suzerainty of Hastinapura. Drupada returned to Kampilya, angry, brooding, plotting revenge. For friendship between kings of neighbouring kingdoms, is not as the friendship between companions. Many years later, Drupada's son Drishtadyumna would be Kutaja's sworn enemy who would

---

[61] Two neighbouring kings cannot be friends, a point made in the Arthashastra by Kautilya. So Drupada's statement does not mean that he wants to be friends with his new neighbour Kutaja ruling from Ahicchatra – it means exactly the opposite! Meanwhile, Kutaja's options are limited – he can kill his childhood friend Drupada and take over his kingdom, or he can leave Drupada as king of one half of a divided kingdom and maintain a delicate peace between the two. Kutaja chooses the second option out of a hope that there would be no war and in a few generations, the divisions might disappear.

kill Kutaja. His daughter Draupadi would bring down Hastinapura.

On that day, Kutaja, son of Bharadvaja, master of weaponry, set in motion the events that would culminate in the Great War that was to destroy the ancient world of Jambudvipa, the continent of the rose-apple tree.

Karna

KARNA

AN UNINVITED CHALLENGER

Everybody turned towards the entrance to the arena for there was renewed cheering and yelling. Something was happening.

It was late afternoon and the tournament was winding down. It had been an exciting day for the crowds and the people had received their fill of circuses. Before lunch there was the excitement of the Suyodhana-Bhima mace fighting demonstration that had not seemed like a demonstration at all. The spectators in the cheap seats in the back couldn't make out much but the pace and fury of the duel grabbed their attention. Even the old soldier who kept the children occupied with his stories of the days of King Shantanu's father, when the tournament included a genuine no-holds-barred battle between a bunch of rakshasas[62] who had been taken prisoner and three Persian lions, stopped talking. People watched and then looked at Kutaja to see if he would stop the bout. He didn't and the bout became more and more ferocious. Then the teacher's son, a young lad named Aswatthama, intervened to stop the bout. Then a glancing hit pushed Aswatthama to the ground and the roar of the crowd rose higher and higher and louder and louder until it reached the fighters. Bhima and Suyodhana stopped swinging and rested on their maces. Aswatthama got up, bruised but unharmed. The crowd cheered. Bhima and Suyodhana then walked off the field without looking at each other. The crowd fell silent.

After lunch, the excitement grew. Everybody expected something spectacular. The crowd stood and cheered when Kutaja, the teacher, bow in hand ran into the arena. A target had been set up all the way across from the entrance. The first one hit the target in the centre and the crowd cheered. It was an amazing shot, at a hundred yards from one end of the arena to the other. The second arrow was shot to

A Tournament

---

[62] Phonetic: Rāxəśə; Syllabic: (I)Raq-shu(dder)-su(h);

the right, but by some miracle of the wind, or perhaps magic, it was racing towards the target and it hit the end of the first one. The crowd gasped and then cheered. They had never seen anything like this. A third arrow shot to the left similarly turned towards the target and hit the end of the second arrow. Like a boomerang, the fourth arrow shot away from the target turned back and hit the third arrow. The crowd stopped cheering, awed into silence by this display. Five more arrows, making for one in each of the eight directions. In stunned silence the crowd watched them embed into each other. Then Kutaja held his arms out acknowledging the crowd and they roared.

Kutaja walked into the centre of the arena. He raised his arms and the crowd became silent, waiting for another marvel. He announced, "My pupil, the young and accomplished Arjuna, son of Pandu and Kunti, equal to the god Indra in his strength and presence will now show his skill."

Arjuna, young and oh, so handsome, came into the arena in his chariot headed straight for the teacher. When it seemed that he could not avoid hitting Kutaja, the charioteer had pulled the horses to the right and Arjuna went past his teacher, hands joined in greeting. He raced around the arena, shooting arrows towards all sections of the field. A bale of hay behind the target was the first to be hit. The bale burst into flame for the arrow was no mere arrow, it was the Agney-astra, the fire-missile. The

second arrow, evidently a Varuna-astra, the water-missile, extinguished the fire; the rising smoke was dispersed with the Vayavy-astra, the wind-missile, and then a cooling rain had fallen on the crowd with the Paarjany-astra. He had created a mirage with the Bhoumya-astra of a glorious land near enough to be reached and then with the Parvata-astra he had created mountains that made that land inaccessible. Finally, with the Anthardhyan-astra he dissolved all the effects he had created with the other weapons.

A Moving Target

The astras were weapons that could only be used in unusual circumstances. They were magical, said to be of divine origin. Magic took time and each astra had to be prepared individually. Some astras took weeks and months of preparation. A Brahma-astra could take years, maybe even an entire lifetime. Astras were rarely used.

The premier weapon of the mounted Kshatriya warrior was the bow and arrow – they required very little preparation. Arjuna showed his skill and accuracy by shooting at an iron pig that was being moved about while he rode around the arena and by shooting at a horn swaying by a rope from a tall pole. From the crowd's reaction, Arjuna had equalled the feats of his teacher.

The demonstration over, people began leaving. The yelling and cheering from the entrance was unexpected. There was consternation in the royal box at the sound of a chariot being ridden at full tilt and the twang of a bowstring. Everybody looked to the entrance.

The cheering rose to a roar as a man appeared at the entrance to the arena. His body shone with golden armour, as brilliant as the setting sun, that he wore as though he and the armour were unified. The man raised his bow high and twanged it again. A Mystery
Suyodhana watched the display and the sound thrilled him as though this was the friend who had come to save him; the same sound raised a pang of foreboding in Yudhishthira. The newcomer turned to look at the royal box. Kunti saw the earrings and the armour on his body and fainted – her brother-in-law Vidura held her while her maids set cool wash-cloths on her face. Kunti came to and looked around confused. Then her eyes focused on the arena and comprehension dawned. She saw the golden man and fainted again.

The Mahabharata does not tell us how many times Vidura had to revive her, but it does tell us that the sight of this warrior overwhelmed her. Could he be the baby she had given up so many years ago? The secret she had nurtured for such a long time. He was glorious in appearance. It had to be him. This reminder of what she had done constricted her throat and she grew faint with foreboding and sorrow and happiness.

The young man saluted the king and his entourage. Then he turned to the public and he proclaimed, "O, Arjuna! You have done great and wonderful feats. Whatever you have done, I shall do better right now. Everybody shall see that you are not so unique after all." Then he turned back to the royal box and addressed Kutaja, "Wise Teacher! This is your arena. Do I have your permission?"

As Kutaja considered, the crowd's rumbling grew and grew

and grew. "Let him!" they chanted. The chants grew louder. Kutaja looked towards Dhritarashtra. Vidura left Kunti and whispered into the blind king's ear, "A challenger has come into the arena. He offers to copy all of Arjuna's feats. He looks young but is also skilled at controlling the chariot."

Blind as Dhritarashtra was, it was not difficult to interpret the emotions that played across his face – his sons had not distinguished themselves that day; Bhima and Arjuna, especially Arjuna, were being celebrated as champions; here was somebody who could show them up. Dhritarashtra nodded his head. "He has my permission. May the crowd be pleased."

Skilled Archery

Kutaja turned back and raised his hands in permission. Then the man accomplished every one of the feats that Arjuna had. He did better than that. Where Arjuna had shot the iron pig while riding clockwise, the mysterious archer did it both clockwise and counter-clockwise; he replaced the horn swaying on a tall pole with a spinning horn and nailed it with a short arrow. The crowds cheered him. The Pandavas stood at their places, trying to look unmoved by the spectacle of Arjuna being over-shadowed by this stranger.

Suyodhana was overwhelmed with joy. This man was making Arjuna look like a child, showing up the Pandavas for the fools they were. When the man was finished, he turned to the royal box and joined his hands. Then he turned to the audience and raised his arms and the crowd roared their approval. The Pandavas stayed quiet. Suyodhana ran out to the chariot, jumped into it and embraced him, and said, "You are magnificent. You shall be my friend."

The man replied, "O prince! What greater joy can fate hold for me than your friendship? What is there beyond that friendship that I could desire? Yes, I will be your friend. First, I want to duel Arjuna. Now."

AN UNFIT CHALLENGER!

Arjuna, who had been discomfited by the man's actions, heard this and was incensed. "You! Uninvited fool with your gold earrings!" he taunted, "Who are you! What kind of uncalled-for boast is this? A duel would give me leave to kill you!"

The man replied, "My name is Vasusena, but I am also called Karna, for my ears are my most distinctive features." He took his helmet off and his ears were large and decorated with gold earrings. The crowd cheered again.

Vasusena continued, "Are your abuses your best weapon, o prince? Are these words the best you can do? Words are the whine of the weak, the whimper of the powerless. One who follows the warrior's Dharma bows before strength, not words. If you have strength you will talk with weapons and arrows. Then we shall see my arrows subdue yours and take your head to your ancestors in front of your teacher."

Arjuna looked at Kutaja for permission. Kutaja, who had become increasingly irritated with this newcomer, nodded in assent to the duel. The arena was cleared. Arjuna and the man faced each other, conscious that this day might leave one of them dead. With stoic demeanour, they assessed each other. The evening

A Duel

sun's rays reflected off the golden armour and the man blazed like a second sun. Beside him, Arjuna looked like the boy that he was and the crowd fell silent. Arjuna, sometimes called the Black Prince in humor, glowered at the man and his glare was a monsoon cloud that would mask the sun.

Kunti fainted again, and Vidura splashed her with sandalwood water and revived her yet again. Now she was in agony, for the matter had gone beyond her grasp.

Kutaja came onto the field between the two combatants who had prepared their bows and arrows. "To my right," he announced, "is the third son of the late King Pandu, called Jishnu at birth by his royal father, known as Arjuna for the complexion of his skin and Savyasachi[63] by those who know him. His father is a Kaurava of the royal family of Hastinapura and his mother is Prtha, daughter of Kuntibhoja. His lineage is great and distinguished."

He turned to the man, "You, sir, must now acquaint us with your name and lineage. Who are your father and mother? What is your lineage? What qualifies you to issue this challenge?"

The man stood silent. His golden blaze seemed to fade as

---

[63] Suvyasachi, pronounced Su(m)-vee-yah-sah-chi, means ambidextrous.

though a monsoon cloud had indeed been pulled across the face of the sun. Slowly, his eyes stopped glaring at Arjuna, glanced briefly at the teacher and fell to the ground. His shoulders slumped and his body's golden cover faded. Kunti's heart leaped for she wanted to jump up and claim this one as her own, but some coldly calculating internal demon would not let her and she watched as the man's brilliance abated.

Suyodhana leaped out of his seat in anger. "What does it matter that he was not born a king? He can become one by leading an army to victory. He can have kingship bestowed upon him by one qualified to do so. I, King of Anga by right, anoint him in my stead as king there. Come, O brahmins, I wish to perform the coronation ritual here and now." Right there in the middle of that crowded arena and in the presence of the nobles and elders and teacher of the Kuru kingdom, Duryodhana crowned the man. When asked his name, the now popular man said "Vasusena." Then after a pause he said, "Crown me as Vasusena, but as a warrior I will be called Karna." The crowd roared with laughter. The duel would be a splendid culmination of an extraordinary day. Karna turned to Suyodhana and asked, "What can I give you in return that would match this gift of a kingdom?" to which Suyodhana replied, "Your eternal friendship." Thus, right then and there, Karna, the eldest brother of the Pandavas, sealed a bond of love and friendship with their most implacable enemy.

The crowds continued cheering as the two combatants faced each other again and this time, Karna began, "I am Vasusena Karna, King of …" but before he could complete the sentence, the crowd hushed and was silent for an old man hobbled into the arena supported by a stick. Karna stopped and walked over to the man, for it was the father he had known all his life. "My son, my son," beamed the old man as Karna bowed to him and touched his head to his feet. "I heard you were being crowned."

Tears fell onto the anointed head of the King of Anga as the lame old man raised him to his feet and kissed and embraced his son.

"He is Adhiratha[64]," somebody whispered, "Adhiratha the

---

[64] Phonetic: Adhirəthə; Syllabic: u(h)-thee-ru(t)-thu(d).

suta[65], the wagon driver." And once more a whisper grew into a rumble, the rumble became a roar, and the crowd knew that Karna, the challenger, the King of Anga, was the son of a cart-driver. At that Bhima leaped onto the floor of the arena roaring with laughter.

"Son of an animal-whipper! You have no right to fight a son of Prtha. You have no right to be the King of Anga! A dog has more right to eat the meat and bones left behind at a sacrifice then you do to enjoy the perquisites you have laid claim to today! Run away before we whip you the way you've learned to whip cattle and horses."

Karna looked at Bhima and a shudder passed through his frame. He looked up at the setting sun as if seeking support. Suyodhana leaped to defend his friend. He said:

"Bhima, you fat fool! Birth is a mystery that cannot be resolved by abuse. A kshatriya is one by force of arms. Karna's physique and appearance, his armour, even his earring-adorned ears, show that he is one destined to rule the world, not just Anga. He is not just Karna, he is not just another Raja, he is Rājādhirāja Su-Karna, with beautiful ears."

Suyodhana's angry words pleased the audience and they responded with loud acclamation. Suyodhana, not usually popular, took heart from the support of the crowd.

"If somebody here disagrees with my action in crowning Karna the King of Anga, let him challenge me with bow and mace, not with words and abuse!" When he said this, the sun seemed to lurch and as though it had satisfied its curiosity disappeared behind the western horizon.

In India, when the sun sets, dusk arrives sharply and suddenly. The day is done and the night is a time of rest. The chief referee announced that with the setting of the sun, the tournament was over. The crowds lingered to see if something would come out of the angry exchange of words, but the elders had intervened. Suyodhana holding Karna by the hand and surrounded by his cheering brothers bowed curtly to the elders and left the arena. The crowds followed them and then dissipated. King Dhritarashtra and his entourage left. Kunti had

---

[65] Phonetic: Sūta; Syllabic: Sue-thu(d).

fainted again when it appeared that Arjuna might fight Karna, and had been revived by the indefatigable Vidura, but then had fainted again., when she saw Karna acknowledge the old wagon-driver as his father. Vidura who by now was concerned for her health made sure that she was accompanied to the ladies' quarters and arranged for a doctor to see her. The Pandavas left by themselves, their hearts heavy. Suyodhana had publicly shown enmity to them; he had made a powerful new friend; in their arrogance, they had alienated the crowds and misplayed their hand. Bhima had been outmatched by Suyodhana in their duel and now it appeared to Yudhishthira that Karna was a better bowman than Arjuna.

Knowledge is not Power

KNOWLEDGE IS NOT POWER

KARNA IS STUCK

"Kill him! Kill him now!" said Krishna.

Arjuna hesitated. Karna, who he had been duelling all day, was defenceless. Karna was by the wheel of his chariot that he had been straining to lift out of the mud. At the sound of Krishna's voice commanding Arjuna to kill him, Karna turned and stared at Krishna. Krishna had pulled Arjuna's chariot up alongside Karna's disabled chariot. Karna's charioteer Salya looked down at Karna. Salya's face showed no emotion, as he strained to get the horses under control. It was coming to the end of a long day and the horses needed to rest.

The battlefield had become quiet. The fighting paused. Imagine, if you will, a movie that has stopped at a critical point during the play. Karna felt as though time had stopped – the battlefield had become quiet and all action had frozen around him. Karna watched as Arjuna slowly put an arrow to his bow and slowly, slowly, pulled the bowstring back. Arjuna seemed to hesitate. Krishna made an impatient sound. Karna tried, once again, to remember the Brahma-astra, the magic spell that would release a missile of Universal Destruction. Parashurama had taught him the spell those many years ago. Now his memory failed him.

There was nothing wrong with his memory. He recalled that fateful day. His guru Parashurama was tired and wanted to sleep. Karna sat down and Parashurama rested his head in Karna's lap. Parashurama was old, almost from another age. He slept a lot. He was irritable and easily angered. Karna had not known that when he had gone to Parashurama and begged to be his pupil.

"Why?" asked Parashurama.

"You are the master of all weapons, both mundane and magical," said Karna.

"Many have studied with me. Go to one of them."

Karna hung his head.

"What's the matter?" asked Parashurama. *Why do I have to speak? Why was this boy in golden armour insisting on studying with him?*

"Guru-ji! I cannot go to your other pupils. I am not accepted."

Parashurama looked at the boy. He looked like a kshatriya. He had the carriage of a trained warrior. He even smelled like a kshatriya.

"Why not? My pupil Kutaja teaches kshatriyas."

"I am not a kshatriya. I am a brahmin, a Bhargava, like yourself. Kutaja says that he cannot teach a Bhargava for they are the enemies of kshatriyas, his students. Even though he learned his craft from you, a Bhargava."

"My high-born disciples will not teach Bhargavas, eh?" Parashurama was angry. He was a Bhargava. He had carried out a vendetta against kshatriyas for much of his life to avenge the killing of his mother and father at the hands of kshatriyas. Finally, he had been persuaded to stop. Then the brahmins, who understood the secrets of language and the significance of the whispered word, had flocked to him to learn the martial arts and the magical weapons of which he was the master. There were so many of them. He had refused many of them – he knew that they would all end up in the service of some kshatriya king or the other, selling the skills he had taught them to the highest bidder. The Brahma-astra, his most powerful weapon, had been taught to very few, only the skilled ones who would be able to control it.

Parashurama recalled Kutaja. When Parashurama had been persuaded by the messenger of the gods to end his self-appointed task of cleaning the earth of all kshatriyas, he decided to give away all his possessions and retire to the mountains. On the selected day, brahmins had come one by one until everything was gone. Just as he was getting ready to leave, Kutaja had arrived. There was nothing left to give. Kutaja seemed desperate. Parashurama offered him knowledge of divine weapons. It would take six months and Kutaja would have to come to the mountains with him for that time. Kutaja had been reluctant but accepted. That was how Kutaja had obtained the recipe for the Brahma-astra along with other astras.

Parashurama said to Karna, "So who is your father, boy? How

do you come by this armour that clings to you like skin?"

The Mahabharata does not record Karna's answer. Whatever it was, it satisfied Parashurama. The Parashurama that Karna encountered was old. Some days he was coherent. He appeared to be waiting for something, or someone, and until that happened, he would not die. In the meantime, his faculties were failing.

KARNA'S ILL-LUCK

Karna spent the next six months with Parashurama. It was the one time in Karna's life that he had been truly happy. The excitement of challenging Arjuna and being crowned king of Anga had been followed by depression. The people he most wished would include him were the kshatriyas of Hastinapura, but only Suyodhana and his brothers had accepted him without questions. There were costs -- the arrogance of the Kauravas had alienated many but as they were the sons of the king, it was not safe to retaliate against them. However, it was safe to humiliate Karna, the *sutaputra*, the outsider for he could not retaliate. Despite Suyodhana's friendship, because of Suyodhana's friendship, Karna had suffered.

However, in Parashurama's retreat in Mount Mahendra, things were different. Parashurama came to rely on Karna. He was like a sponge and absorbed his teachings immediately. Soon Parashurama had taught Karna all the magical weapons he knew. The only one left to be taught was the Brahma-astra. Parashurama was waiting for the right day.

Karna was normally a bright and sunny man, though occasionally subject to melancholic moods. The other residents in the ashram loved him for he was always helpful. That year game was scarce and one day the residents of the ashram were bemoaning the lack of meat in their diet – Karna decided to go hunting. With his sword strapped on and bow in hand he had gone off into the dense forest that fringed the lake near Mount Mahendra. He heard the growl of a wild beast some distance away and then saw a tiger leap in the brush and hold onto an animal. As the tiger killed the animal, a larger horned creature lumbered away and Karna realized that it must be the companion or parent of the tiger's prey. So he shot his arrows in the direction of the movement. His arrows found their mark and a little later all was quiet. The tiger dragged its prey off and Karna made his way to his kill. It was a cow and not the wild animal he had expected. It clearly belonged to somebody. The owner must have run away when the tiger attacked. As Karna wondered what to do, a brahmin ran up to him – he was a brahmin from the nearby village who performed Vedic rituals for the villagers.

"You killed my cow?" he said, his voice rising in pitch and his body shaking.

"I am sorry," said Karna. "I saw the tiger attack something and thought it was a wild deer."

"What kind of brainless hunter are you? This cow provided milk for me and my family and for the daily performance of rituals. I cannot do without the cow. What am I to do? You stupid killer, you have ruined me."

Karna could not appease him at all.

"You have undone me, you wicked man! You look like a brahmin, so I will not curse you to die. You think highly of your martial skills! When you are fighting your greatest enemy, your chariot wheel will be seized by the earth. When you try to disengage from the battle to free your chariot, your enemy will not permit you to withdraw but will attack you and kill you!"

Karna was aghast. His knees threatened to give way. What kind of curse was this? He would die in the most humiliating fashion, weapon-less in battle.

He said, "Please, sir! O! great one! I killed your cow without knowing. I will compensate you many times over. Please ... withdraw your curse! I beg you! Please forgive me! The kings of the world will give you cattle many times over, riches, jewels, whatever you wish! Please forgive my error!"

The brahmin did not relent. The curse was not withdrawn and Karna returned to Parashurama's ashram depressed and frightened.

Karna recalled the curse as Arjuna aimed his arrow at Karna. This was it. The curse had taken effect. Even the sun, who illuminated all and saw everything, had taken refuge behind a cloud. His body slumped as he considered what he could do. His charioteer Salya had been useless, for he continued sitting in his position looking down at him.

I should use the Brahma-astra – it is the only divine weapon I have left. He picked up a blade of grass.

Another shred of memory, of the day he learned the Brahma-astra, intervened. The Brahma-astra was a difficult weapon to teach and difficult weapon to learn for even a single mistake could be catastrophic. Especially while teaching – an unprepared student could release it and not be able to rein it back. After teaching Karna the brahmastra, and pleased with his student's facility, Parashurama felt tired. "Come, dear boy, sit here and let me put my head on your lap for a little time," he said. As soon as he laid his head down he had fallen asleep on Karna's lap.

A large deer-fly landed on his thigh by the guru's head. Karna had sat absolutely still, for if he moved, the guru would wake up and be unhappy that his rest was disturbed. Though Parashurama loved Karna, he would also scold him constantly when he was upset. Karna hoped that the fly would leave, but then the fly bit into his thigh. It was a sharp sting, but he felt he could handle it without moving – after all he had suffered worse in innumerable practice bouts.

Then the fly started burrowing into his flesh, tearing off bits of muscle. The wound grew and more blood appeared. Karna gritted his teeth against the pain. He was a kshatriya; he would not give in to the pain. He maintained his calm but the insect must have struck a vein for blood started pouring out of the wound. There was nothing he could do but watch as the stream of blood ran over Parashurama's face.

The warm blood collecting on the side of his face woke Parashurama. He felt the blood and then saw where it came from. Karna was sitting stoically, his eyes closed, while blood streamed down his thigh.

I have been lied to, he thought. He sat up.

"Karna! What is this blood?"

Karna moved and the fly flew away. It was a relief, but he was happy that Parashurama had been able to rest. If only the fly had not bitten him – Karna was apologetic.

"A fly bit me, guru-ji. I did not want to disturb you, so I did not wave it away. It was nothing sir. I am sorry that your sleep was disturbed."

Parashurama was not mollified.

"You are no brahmin. Only a kshatriya would bear such a wound without crying. You are a kshatriya! You lied to me!"

Karna stared blankly at his guru. *What to do?*

Parashurama continued.

"Look at this wound! Look at all the blood! Only a kshatriya would be stupid enough to bear such a wound without a murmur. If you were a brahmin, you would have been screaming your head off. You are no merchant. If you were a low-caste *Parayan*, you would have killed the insect as soon as it landed on you, without considering the disturbance it might have created for me. Only the stupid warriors would do this. Who are you? Tell me the truth or I shall kill you right now!"

Karna swallowed. "I am a suta, the son of Adhiratha, a caretaker of horses in Hastinapura," he said.

"Why did you lie to me? Why did you tell me that you were a brahmin?" Parashurama had stood up and was looking down at Karna. His shoulders and hands were shaking, his face was red, and his frail body seemed ready to explode.

"I wanted to learn all of the divine weapons that Kutaja refused to teach me. I knew that you would teach me only if I was not a kshatriya."

"So that was why you came to me. I have been an old fool who was taken in by your pleasant smile and youth. You say you are not a kshatriya, so I will not kill you. You know that the Brahma-astra is reserved for brahmins only. You had no right to it."

"Forgive me!" Karna had fallen to the feet of his guru, abasing himself in the fashion that was already traditional at that time. Tears rolled down his eyes, of sorrow, of self-pity, of chagrin.

"You have been a good pupil, but I cannot let you have the brahma-astra. I cannot make you unlearn it. But it shall not benefit you, ever. I curse you – when you face your greatest opponent and you need this weapon, your memory will fail you. You will be unable to use this weapon when you most need it."

Karna hung his head.

"Go! Get out of my sight!"

Parashurama stalked off.

KARNA'S END

Karna's last memory, of Parashurama as he turned a disgusted face away, bubbled to the top as he faced Arjuna and Krishna. *One curse had already taken effect. Was it time for the second one?* Arjuna still hesitated. Krishna seemed to look at Karna as though he knew his deepest secrets. The brahmastra spell refused to form on Karna's lips. As he struggled with it, he heard Krishna's clear voice.

Krishna said, "He is trying to release the brahmastra. If he succeeds, you are lost. He looks like he is getting ready to release it!. Kill him before he recovers."

Karna tried to stop the inevitable once more. "Arjuna! Would you kill an unarmed man? I have put down my weapons. I am trying to free my chariot. You, who know the rules of single combat, know that killing me now, in this manner, would forever be a stain on your reputation. Let me free my chariot and we can resume our battle."

Arjuna hesitated, for Karna was echoing the debate going on in his mind. Krishna argued against Karna's proposal.

"Arjuna, do not listen to this evil man. He is simply angling for time."

Then Krishna faced Karna and said, "O, Karna! This is certainly an opportune time for you to bring up the rules of war. Tell me, by what rules did you and the Kauravas cause the slaughter of Abhimanyu? Suyodhana and the rest of the Kauravas loudly proclaimed how they had surrounded the boy and killed him. You were part of that crowd that broke his bow, cut down his chariot, and killed his horses and charioteer. Then, while he stood defenceless in the field of battle, you attacked him, not even one at a time, but as a mob."

The entire battlefield had come to a halt when Karna and Krishna exchanged these words. The Pandava warriors felt a resurgence of spirit and anger at Krishna's words; the Kauravas were chagrined at this public denunciation of their tactics in killing Abhimanyu.

Krishna continued, "Arjuna! Kill him now. Do not hesitate. He is a dead man and only awaits your arrow to free his spirit from his body."

Arjuna released a crescent-shaped arrow. Karna held his head high – he would not bow in the face of death. *I accept it. If it must be, so be it.* Moving swiftly, the fateful arrow lopped off Karna's head from his body.

Salya, Karna's charioteer, had promised Yudhishthira that he would belittle Karna to make him lose heart in his final battle with Arjuna. Salya had delivered on his promise, but he had not expected Arjuna to kill Karna in this manner. He had not expected the advice that Krishna gave. He had not expected his nephew to violate the rules of war in this manner.

Salya said, "Krishna! Arjuna! What you just did does not bode well. Your victory violates Dharma. You should have known better." He went down and picked up Karna's body and loaded it into the chariot. Miraculously, with Karna's death the chariot wheels had become unstuck. Salya took Karna's body back to the Kaurava camp. It was late in the day but that day the fighting did not stop with the sunset but continued well into the night. There were no rules anymore. The just war had descended into just chaos.

EKALAVYA

Ekalavya

A dark boy with a broad flat nose stood quietly by the door. He had by his side a bow and a quiver filled with arrows. Unlike the decorated and elegantly shaped bows of the nobility, his bow appeared to have been built with slats of hand-cut wood tied with coir rope. His arrows seemed to have been cut and trimmed by himself. He did not look older than eight years of age, but he stood silently and attentively without fidgeting.

The door opened and Kutaja's wife Kripi looked out. She usually came out in the early dawn to decorate the entrance to her home and make it a welcome place to visit. "You are still here?" she asked when she saw the boy, "Why did you not see the Teacher in his school?"

Boy waiting

"The other boys would not let me in. I am Ekalavya, son of Hiranyadhanus. My father may be the chief of the Nishadas but I am of no account here as I am neither brahmin nor kshatriya." His voice broke and his lower lip trembled as he said the last phrase but he kept his poise.

"How awful for you!" Kripi sympathized. "These children may be the children of nobles but they have not learned nobility. Not at all like their grandfather Shantanu. Shantanu found my brother Kripa and me abandoned in the forest and straightaway adopted us as foster children. We could be Naga or Nishada, even Rakshasa! It did not matter! Now Kripa is a respected teacher of weaponry and I too know the use of weapons. Nobody refused to teach us because we were not noble or because our caste was unknown!"

"The Teacher is still asleep," continued Kripi, "He will be up soon for his morning ritual. I will ask him to see you then."

The boy waited. Half an hour later, Kutaja came out and looked at the boy. He looked at the slight figure and his shabby clothes. He looked at the bow and the arrows and frowned. "You are the boy?" he asked gruffly.

Ekalavya smiled, his white teeth sparkling against his dark

face. "Yes, Teacher."

"You wish to learn from me?"

"Yes, Teacher."

"Come with me." Kutaja led him to the archery field in which a target had been set up. "Shoot four arrows at that target."

Ekalavya lifted his bow above his head, nocked the arrow, pulled the bowstring and brought it down to aim. Kutaja interrupted, "Before you let go of the arrow, tell me, what do you see."

"I see a red dot," said the boy.

"Anything else," asked Kutaja, surprised by the answer. Kripi was right, this boy was special.

"No."

"You may shoot."

Rapidly, Ekalavya shot four arrows as commanded. The first one hit the bull's eye in the center and the rest lodged one after the other in the feathers of the previous arrow. The boy turned to Kutaja and bowed. He then awaited further instructions a happy smile playing on his face.

Kutaja stood deep in thought. He regretted having brought the boy here to test. If only he had been like the others who came to him, it would have been easy to dismiss him. Unfortunately, it was not so. The boy was perfectly disciplined. His walk to the field had been an exercise in precision. His bow, however different, had been handled with pride and respect. His eyesight was perfect and his focus was immaculate. Even his stoic patience hinted at his potential as a warrior. He was the perfect pupil.

Unfortunately, he was a Nishada and he could become a greater archer than Arjuna. He, Kutaja, had promised Arjuna, his favourite pupil, that he would be the best archer in the world. He had no doubt that if Ekalavya became his pupil, he would surpass Arjuna.

He was a Nishada and he would amount to nothing in the world dominated by Kshatriyas.

Kutaja made his decision. He shook his head. "You may go

now. I cannot accept you in my school."

Ekalavya's smile disappeared. His face fell. He was only eight and though he had bravely put up with the arrogant slights and taunts of the city-dwellers, he had not expected this.

"Why? Why can't you teach me?" the question came out as a croak.

Kutaja avoided answering him. "There is no reason. I choose not to accept you in my school. You may leave now."

The boy's eyes lost their sparkle and his shoulders slumped. He stood there as though uncertain. He looked around his eyes darting looking for something to stare at. He saw the two stone figurines at the entrance to the field representing Brihaspati the teacher of the gods and Sukra the teacher of the asuras. The boy recalled that Brihaspati's son Kacha had studied under Sukra, despite repeated attempts to dissuade him. He, Ekalavya, did not intend to be dissuaded by a single "No." from the guru he wanted. He straightened his spine, looked at Kutaja and said, "Thank you, Teacher," and walked out of the field without a single backward glance.

Kutaja shook his head. *It is sad, but I will not break the rule.* He went back to his house to get ready for the day.

Five years passed. Once a week, Kutaja excused the students from practice and they would often go into the forest to hunt at leisure. The Pandavas had gone with a bearer and his dog. They had left the rest of their attendants in a forest grove to set up camp while they walked around. When they had gone some distance, they heard the dog barking loudly. Concerned that there might be an intruder they started back but were startled when the dog's barking ended in a long, drawn-out howl. They rushed back to the campsite where they were confronted with the dog lying on the ground with its mouth full of arrows. The bearer was in shock – when the dog started barking he had followed the dog until they came to the end of a trail. The forest was not passable there, but the dog had smelled something and had continued barking. Suddenly the arrows had flown in through the bush and lodged in the dog's mouth. Then there was silence.

Frightened, the bearer had picked up the dog and returned to

The barking dog

the campsite waiting for the Pandavas. Arjuna was impressed, "All these arrows are from the same archer – see how uniform the arrows are. Also, all the arrows are notched the same way. Truly, this is a master of the bow."

The bearer led them to the trail and when they came to the end of the trail, they looked for a way across the thicket. They took out their falchions and hacked their way around the place where the arrows had come through. They came through to a grove where a Nishada was exercising with a bow and arrows. They marvelled at the speed with which the Nishada was firing his arrows and his unerring accuracy. When the Nishada saw them, he stopped. With a bow, he said "O! Princes of Hastinapura! Welcome to my home." He gestured to the open arena.

Arjuna, who could not brook a competitor in archery, could barely contain his curiosity. "Who are you? Where did you learn to shoot like that? Who is your teacher?"

The Nishada smiled with a smile that lit up his face. "My name is Ekalavya and I am the son of Hiranyadhanus, the chief of the Nishadas. You do not know me for your rulers do not mingle with us. Your people have seen me many times and know me well enough."

He continued, "I learned to shoot like that by incessant practice. For the last five years, I have practiced archery under the tutelage of the best weapons master in the world, Kutaja."

Yudhishthira saw Arjuna flinch. He was struggling to control his fury and disappointment. He pulled Arjuna to the side. Bhima who had also seen Arjuna's reaction, took over the conversation with the Nishada, while Arjuna sulked. There was not much to be said, for the Nishada was properly deferential with them. He knew who they were, smiled frequently, and behaved respectfully to the princes.

When the Pandavas returned to Hastinapura, they described the Nishada to Kutaja and were curious about this secret disciple of his, for Kutaja had never mentioned Ekalavya and Ekalavya had never come to the regular school. Kutaja kept silent. When all the students had left, having said their farewells for the day to Kutaja, Arjuna stayed behind, his pale face darkened, his eyes sparkling, and his chest trembling. Kutaja went to him and would have embraced him, but Arjuna stepped away. He spoke furiously, his love for his teacher battling the disappointment and jealousy raging in his heart.

"You embraced me and told me once that I would be your best pupil. That no pupil of yours would excel me. Even when you accepted Karna as a student, you told me in private that Karna would never be a better warrior than me. Now, I find that the son of a Nishada chief can easily best me. What is the value of your promise?"

Kutaja looked at Arjuna, beautiful and blazing in his anger. He did not know how to address this problem. He had failed in his promise to Arjuna. *What can I do?* His shoulders slumped and he looked around, uncertain. His eyes fell on the figurines of Brihaspati, the teacher of the gods, and Sukra, the teacher of the asuras, that graced the entrance to the practice hall. The asura king's jealousy over Sukra's daughter's love for Kacha, Brihaspati's son, had led them to kill Kacha and feed him to Sukra. That very excess had forced Sukra to restore Kacha to life, teach him the secret knowledge he had come for, and break his daughter's heart. He, Kutaja, would have to do something to prevent Arjuna's jealousy poisoning his life.

"Take me to Ekalavya," he said, taking Arjuna by the hand.

Arjuna led him to Ekalavya's home in the forest. When Ekalavya saw Kutaja and Arjuna, he beamed. His smile was radiant – it was as though the sun had risen again and had lighted up the small cottage. "I am fortunate," he said, "I knew that when I encountered the Pandavas today, the day was not far off when I would again be graced with your presence, o, Teacher!" He bowed deeply to Kutaja and paid him obeisance appropriate to a Teacher. He acknowledged Arjuna's presence in a manner appropriate to a fellow pupil in the presence of their teacher.

Kutaja said, "Tell me, Ekalavya! How long have you been my pupil and how have you been receiving my instruction?"

Ekalavya replied, "Five years ago, you said that you could not accept me in your school. I could see from the look in your face that you were not rejecting me as your pupil. I saw the statues of Brihaspati and Sukracharya and realized that a teacher could teach in more ways than one. Thus!" He pointed to a shrine in a corner of the practice hall that contained a clay figure with a neat beard and a top-knot.

"You have been present at all my practices in that form."

Arjuna was taken aback. He wondered how this Nishada had managed to become so skilled when practicing with an effigy.

Ekalavya continued, "I would climb a tree on the edge of your school grounds and watch what you taught the students during the day. Then in the evening and at night I would return here and practice those same moves by myself, under your guidance. Thus, I became as skilled as any of your pupils. Only on the days that you gave your pupils leisure did I practice during the day and that is why I had the great fortune to meet the generous Yudhishthira, the powerful Bhima, and the great-hearted Arjuna. They are my heroes."

Learning from afar

Arjuna winced. He wished he had stayed behind, and let Kutaja come by himself. Kutaja kept hold of Arjuna's hand.

"Prince of the Nishadas," said Kutaja, "It has been several years since you started this regimen under me. You have become a master."

The boy's relaxed. "Thank you, sire! I am glad that I have not displeased you."

"I have come for my guru-dakshina."

Ekalavya smiled, an open smile that filled the room with radiance. "My heart is full. You ask for what is right and it shall be my gift to you."

Kutaja was blunt, "Your right thumb is my fee."

Ekalavya's smile faltered. Then he reached for his falchion with his left hand and with one swift strike he had lopped off his right thumb. Through the pain of the injury he said, "Teacher! Your fee!" and fainted.

Arjuna stared in shock at the Nishada. Kutaja turned to him. "You are still my best pupil, Arjuna!" he said and walked away from the cottage. At that instant, Arjuna rejoiced at what his teacher had done for him; the next instant, he looked at the bleeding Ekalavya and his mind whirled and his great heart reeled from the shock of witnessing the guru-dakshina.

Arjuna knelt and took Ekalavya's hand in his. It was bleeding profusely and the boy face was pale. Arjuna looked around at the meagre furnishings of the cottage. He ran to a large basket and started rummaging in it. He found

Tuition payment

some pieces of cloth, but they were all too small. Then he found a section of coir rope that had been used to bind a bow. He brought it back and tied a tourniquet around Ekalavya's arm. He held it down until the bleeding stopped. He then used the small pieces of cloth to wrap as a bandage around Ekalavya's thumb. He picked up the boy. "He is so light", he thought in amazement – he would never have been able to pick up Nakula or Sahadeva like this, let alone Bhima. He walked to the Nishada settlement with the boy in his arms.

The Nishada settlement was a collection of thatched wattle-and-daub huts set among trees in a partially cleared section of forest. The trail from the King's Road led to the eastern entrance. The was a guard at the gate. He saluted Arjuna and looked at his burden.

"Where is Hiranyadhanus?" Arjuna said.

The man looked at the body he was carrying in shock.

Arjuna continued, "Please show me the way to his dwelling."

The man turned and ran. Arjuna followed him to a large cottage. A man was coming out. It was Ekalavya's father. Arjuna laid the body at his feet.

The Nishada chief looked mutely at his son. His mouth opened but no sound emerged. Ekalavya's mother came out and started sobbing. The sobs became wails.

"Shh, mother. Ekalavya is not dead." Then he looked at Arjuna, "What happened?"

Arjuna could not speak. He stuttered, "He...he...he..." Then he pointed to the boy's right arm with the cloth bandages and the tourniquet. The father gingerly moved the cloth and saw the bleeding hand. So did the mother and she screamed.

"You did this?" asked the father.

"No." said Arjuna, continuing to stammer, "He...he...he d...d...d...did it hims...s...s...s...self...f..f..f..f."

"You bandaged him," asked the father.

"Yes," said Arjuna and bowed his head.

"Please stay until he wakes up."

Arjuna's voice had returned. "No. You should get a doctor soon for him to stop the bleeding. It is late and my brothers are expecting me back. They will worry."

"Yes, it is late. Please come back tomorrow. You may have saved his life. What he owes you will be difficult to repay."

This was not what Arjuna expected. His head hung even lower. "I must go now," he mumbled and he left the presence of Ekalavya's father and ran all the way home.

Respect

RESPECT

BHIMA AND THE MONKEY

The exiled Pandavas had settled down for a few weeks by a lake-side ashram where many rishis lived. Arjuna had gone off in search of weapons from the gods and the rest of the Pandavas had agreed to wait for him. It was early in the morning, a warm spring day. It was a pleasant and beautiful setting. The lake was fed by many brooks coming

Draupadi

down from the not-too-distant Himalayas. Draupadi and Bhima were alone on the bank of one of these brooks. They were enjoying the scenery, when Draupadi saw a saugandhika flower, a lotus with a thousand petals, shining white and gold, floating down the brook. "Bhima, look!" she exclaimed. "What a beautiful flower. Can you fetch it for me?"

"Of course, love," said Bhima, as he stepped into the water and fetched the flower. Draupadi smiled at him and turned her head. Bhima reached over and slowly inserted the flower into her flowing hair. She turned to him and Bhima was struck with amazement at how the white flower contrasted and enhanced her beauty.

"I want a whole bucket of these flowers," said Draupadi. "I wonder where they came from."

"It cannot be too far from here. The flower was fresh and intact, so it cannot have travelled far. I'll fetch a plant for you today."

Later the morning call for breakfast sounded and Draupadi got up in response. Bhima said, "I am not hungry yet! I'll go get the plant now, my love." He strapped on his sword, shouldered a quiver of arrows, and picked up his bow. Draupadi smiled goodbye and Bhima left, following the brook upstream.

Bhima expected that as he went upstream and higher up the foothills, the forest would become sparser and the going would be easier. He was surprised by what he discovered. After rising a short distance, he entered a heavily forested plateau. Following the brook got harder – the stream flowed faster and deeper. It became harder and harder to stay near the brook for the ground was marshy and not firm. The forest on the bank was dense and he had to use his sword to cut his way through the under growth. Finally, he decided to go further away from the brook and navigate by its sound.

Bhima continued in this manner for almost three hours. The morning was almost up. Even though the forest provided him shade, the heat and humidity and the lack of any wind made it tough going. He was beginning to be hungry and irritable, but before he sat down to eat something, anything really, he wanted to see how much further he would have to go. He climbed a tall tree and looked in the direction that he expected the brook to go.

He was pleasantly surprised. The brook appeared to be coming out from a nearby lake. A quarter of the lake seemed to be covered with lotuses. He saw signs of a walking trail leading to the lake only a short distance from his tree.

Bhima was tired from all the hard work of cutting through the forest. The sight of the lake and the trail to the lake energized him and he ran to the trail and then started running along it. He was so pleased that he started singing. I will not tell you what song he sang or anything else about it, except to note that you would have understood why Bhima was not known for his prowess at singing.

J Suddenly, Bhima was brought to a halt by the sight of a large aged monkey sleeping by the side of the trail. The monkey's tail lay across the trail and Bhima, who was usually polite when it came to older beings felt that he should not show disrespect by crossing over the tail.

The tail was in his way

"Excuse me, sir," he said.[66]

The monkey did not respond. It seemed to be fast asleep. Bhima looked at the tail to see if he could bypass it by going off

---

[66] A digression is in order here. Why was Bhima addressing a monkey? From a rational point of view, there is no evidence that monkeys ever spoke a language, let alone a human language. In Indian mythology, some animals speak – bears, monkeys, snakes, elephants, eagles, and so on. Not all animals, though. Horses, for instance never speak. Neither do cows, goats, sheep, cats, dogs, among others. Certain animals speak only in dreams – cows, some birds, deer. Yet another class of animals have single ideal instances that speak, while all the rest remain silent. An intriguing observation is that the speaking animals are also the ones portrayed on Indus Valley seals. The animals on the Indus seals may have represented fraternal organizations (possibly the prototypes for guilds in a later era).

the trail, but it seemed to be quite a long tail. Also, the monkey was kind of big and its arms were stretched across. In any case, Bhima was tired of hacking at trees and branches and did not want to do so if he could simply use the trail.

"Excuse, me sir," he said, a bit louder. "Could you move your tail?"

There was no response. Now he was getting irritated.

"Excuse me, sir," he said, a lot louder. In fact, I hate to say this, because Bhima was usually so polite, but he shouted this quite close to the monkey.

That got a response. The monkey opened an eye. Then it opened both eyes and yawned.

"Darn it!" said the monkey. "First somebody sings like an owl, and then somebody shouts at me. What do you want?"

"Move your tail off the trail, please!" Bhima was back to being a bit polite.

"Why?" asked the monkey.

"So that I can continue on my way," said Bhima. "I would not want to show disrespect for you by stepping over your body."

"That is certainly thoughtful of you. It is alright though – you are a strong and apparently healthy human and I am only a monkey. Go ahead and step across my tail."

"I can't do that. Please move your tail."

"I am old," said the monkey. "I am also tired, which is why I was asleep. You see how big that tail is. It's a real problem for me when I must move, dragging that tail. I can't move it. You must step over it."

"I won't do that. You must move it."

"Well, I can't, and that's that."

Bhima looked at the monkey in frustration. The monkey looked back at him calmly. Unlike the other Pandavas, Bhima felt a kinship with the creatures of the wild. Unlike Arjuna and Krishna he would never have burned down a forest. Unlike Yudhishthira, he would never have gambled away elephants and horses. He preferred walking to riding. He was called Vrikodara, the wolf-bellied, because of his appetite, but the name made him feel at one with wolves and other forest creatures. He really did not want to show disrespect for this monkey. He had to cross and he did not want to retreat. He had to go across. He growled in frustration. The monkey smiled and growled back.

"Jump over it." said the monkey.

Bhima tried reason. "The universal soul, Brahman, pervades you as much as it pervades me. If you had not been a thinking creature, I would have jumped over you as my brother Hanuman jumped over the ocean."

"Who is this Hanuman who leaped over the ocean? Why did he do it?" asked the monkey.

Bhima was proud of his brother. "Like me, he is the son of Vayu the wind. He was like you, a monkey. He had intelligence, strength, courage, and initiative. To find Rama's wife, he leaped the ocean to Ravana's Lanka. I wish I had the time to tell you the story, but I don't. Let me through. Yes, like my brother, I could leap, but I will not. You must move."

The monkey laughed for it was clear that Bhima did not particularly know the story of Hanuman. "In my sick and old condition, I cannot be like your brother and leap around. Maybe you can. I doubt it though – Hanuman was a monkey and probably stronger than you for you are only a man. Too bad."

Bhima knew what it felt to be made fun of – Duryodhana and his brothers used to tease him as a child. The monkey was making fun of him! He took out his sword and said, "I am a kshatriya, a warrior, a Kuru of the dynasty of the moon. I will not jump over you but I must have my way. Fight me!"

The monkey looked at him. "How would it benefit you, o great warrior, to fight an old monkey like me. Do you see any weapons here? I could not fight you even if I wanted to, and I don't. No, no! If you must cross, you must cross, and I must let you!"

Bhima felt relieved. It appeared that the monkey was going to be reasonable after all.

The monkey continued, "Why don't you just move my tail off the trail? Then you can continue on your way to perform your urgent errand! I am sure it must be something truly important for a great human warrior like you to be in such a hurry!"

Bhima did not like it one bit. He was certain that his leg was being pulled. How could the monkey know the nature of his errand – that was a bit of a mystery? No matter, all he had to do was move the tail.

He bent down and picked up the tail. *Uff!* The tail did not move. It seemed to be stuck to the ground. He looked at the monkey who seemed to have gone back to sleep. He felt under the tail and managed to get his fingers down there. No, there was no glue and the tail was not stuck to the ground. He tried again. No luck! It was a heavy tail.

He moved his fingers underneath the tail across the trail. It wasn't stuck anywhere. Suddenly the tail moved and shivered of its own accord. He looked at the monkey who had now opened an eye. The monkey protested, "That tickled. Just get on with it, o powerful warrior!"

Bhima frowned. He got his hand under the tail and bent his knees and with all his strength he pulled up. Slowly he managed to get it to his thighs and then to his belly and then to his shoulder. The tail was heavy! Slowly, with the tail across his shoulders, he started to move. Then his feet slipped on a leaf and in an instant he was on the ground and the tail was lying across his stomach. It was a heavy tail.

"What's the matter, kshatriya?" said the monkey. "Can't you lift a little old monkey's tail?"

Bhima glowered. "I'll come and move you."

"You know," said the monkey, "When I first saw you I thought you might be Bhima the Pandava who is famous for his strength. I have heard descriptions of him and you match those descriptions. Hmm… though you look like him and your body is built like a wrestler's, it doesn't seem likely that you could hold up a candle to him."

"I am Bhima," growled Bhima.

"Really," said the monkey. "What are you doing here? Where are your brothers and your wife? If you were Bhima they would be nearby. However, you are alone. And you don't seem very strong at all."

"I'll move you," threatened Bhima.

"You could not move my tail, and now you are going to move

me? Sounds a bit unlikely, eh?" said the monkey.

Bhima glared and crawled out from under the tail and tried a second time. He failed again. A third, then a fourth time. Many times, until the sweat poured down his brow and his arms ached and he felt a pain in his shoulder that he had never felt before. Finally, exhausted, he looked at the monkey. This was no monkey. There must be some magic and he had been humbled.

Bhima bowed to the monkey. "Forgive me for having insulted you. What are you, a god or other denizen of heaven? What is your true shape and why have you chosen to test me?"

The monkey smiled. "I will tell you what you must know, o Bhima. I am your brother Hanuman, born of Vayu and the monkey Anjana. I was friends with Sugriva the king of the monkeys who was helped by Rama to regain his kingdom. In turn, Sugriva offered Rama my services to find his wife Sita. I found Sita in Lanka after leaping across the ocean. I confronted Ravana, demanded that he release Sita and when he tried to arrest me, I burnt his city. Then I helped Rama defeat Ravana and regain his wife. In exchange, Rama gave me a boon of my choice and I asked that I live as long as the story of Rama is not forgotten or replaced by a greater story."

Bhima was overjoyed to meet his fabled brother. They hugged and spoke in soft gentle tones. There was so much to find out about each other. Bhima invited Hanuman to come back to the Pandava camp, but Hanuman refused.

Brothers Hug

"I will be with you in spirit," Hanuman said. "If you want me to go and destroy the Kauravas now, I will do it."

Bhima demurred. "My brothers and I have vowed to get our kingdom back from them, but we must win it. Otherwise, there will only be more trouble."

"Yes," said Hanuman. "I understand that it is your kshatriya mind at work. I won't interfere, but I can help. At that final battle, if Arjuna will raise a banner with my image on it, I will add my roar to the sound of your conch and put fear into the hearts of the Kauravas."

Saying this, Hanuman gave his brother a final hug and disappeared.

Bhima, full of joy at having met his brother, raced to the lake to fetch the lotus. He wanted to announce to everybody that he had met his hero, his brother. He was so excited that he splashed water loudly disturbing the crocodiles basking in the sun; the elephant herd come for their midday water hrrumped at him; the monkeys chattered and jumped about. The yaksha guardians of the lake, for it was indeed a lake owned by Kubera, the king of the yakshas, came out and encircled Bhima. He, on the other hand, was so excited that after collecting some flowers and a bunch of plants, he rushed past them back down the trail. The yakshas ran after him, but they were unable to catch him.

Bhima's return with the yakshas following was not a silent affair. The peaceful ascetics of the ashram were concerned that a herd of elephants were stampeding driven by a bull in heat. Yudhishthira wondered where Bhima had gone, for he would have been perfect for stopping such a calamity. He sent the twins who parked themselves across the trail.

Nakula and Sahadeva looked on in amazement at Bhima whooping and yelling as he ran down the trail to the ashram. Behind him were a motley collection of yakshas. Nakula and Sahadeva raised their bows and prepared for battle. When Bhima saw Nakula and Sahadeva getting ready to fight, he stopped.

"What's the matter?"

"The yakshas look like they want a fight," said Nakula.

The yaksha troop had stopped. A commanding presence stepped out from behind them. "Are you Bhima, the Pandava?" he asked.

"Yes."

"We are honoured that you came to visit. For many days, our leader, the god of wealth, Kubera has been awaiting your arrival. He was told that you were headed towards his lands and then you stopped. We were asked to invite you to stay with us, but, alas, we could not even catch up with you! We were beginning to doubt that you were a human and thought you might be a form-changing rakshasa. We would have to fight you then."

Bhima was abashed. He had been so intent on getting the flowers back to Draupadi. He had neglected all the traditional elements of respect. He had not asked permission to pick the flowers from the owner of the lake. He had run away from them when he saw them and though they had pleaded with him to stop he had kept going.

The four Pandavas went on to visit Kubera where they finally got to meet Arjuna on his way back from the Himalayas with divine weapons. Bhima's account of his meeting with his brother Hanuman filled them with wonder. They rejoiced in the new friends they made. Draupadi's desire to smell the fragrance of the lotuses was more than satisfied. As they say, all's well that ends well.

Yakshaprashna

YAKSHAPRASHNA

THE LONG HUNT

"Ha! You missed again, oh great archer!"

Bhima's comment was, Arjuna thought, unhelpful to say the least.

Arjuna said, "Why don't you wrestle it down to the ground?"

His riposte did not make him feel any better. Arjuna and his brothers had been following the stag all morning and he had not even been able to get a clean shot at it.

This inability to capture the stag made Arjuna sensitive to innocent remarks let alone Bhima's charged comments. He thought he knew how to handle frustration – Indra alone knew how it had galled him to hold back from jumping on Duhshasana that day in the dice hall when Draupadi was been dragged by the hair; and how it continued to gall him that his brother  Yudhishthira would not agree to break the agreement to go into exile for twelve years. Today was going badly – he and his brothers had been following the stag all morning and he had not even been able to get a clean shot at it. He was Arjuna, the world's best archer. He could shoot anything that moved or that made a sound. This stag had been different – it had eluded his arrows. It blended into the woods so perfectly he could swear that it was not there and then it would move, challenging him to shoot and by the time he was ready to release the arrow, a fraction of a vighati later, the creature would be invisible again. He had closed his eyes and tried to shoot by sound, but the stag was like an insubstantial ghost that moved silently through the words. Frustrated, he had released a few arrows, wasted them on a mirage and an echo.

The stag ran away

Arjuna's brothers were not doing any better. All five of them had set out to get the stag. It had been early in the morning and they were bored. Even Yudhishthira, who stayed calm all the time looked bored. Yes, they were stressed – their twelve years of exile was about to end. For most of this last year they had lingered at this ashram, making plans for the thirteenth year when they were required to be incognito. They had to be careful of the Kauravas --- they had spies everywhere. All the planning had to be slow, methodical, and deliberate. The evenings had been filled with stories narrated by visitors. The stories had been interesting at first, but they had merely stoked their imaginations and left them with a desire to do something. Anything.

When the ascetic had shouted that he had been attacked by a stag – that in itself was strange as stags did not usually attack people – and that his water jug had been snared in the antelope's horns – an unusual event to say the least – they had all jumped up and said that they were going to hunt down that stag, retrieve the jug, and have venison for lunch that day.

The stag had led them a merry chase and now it was the hottest part of the day. They had rushed out without breakfast and the chase had kept them from lunch. They had not even brought any water, and they were all hungry and thirsty and were snapping at each other. They would feel foolish if they returned without any meat at all, let alone without the stag and the water-jug.

THE LAKE

Yudhishthira called a halt to the hunt. "Nakula! We must have water. Climb that tall tree and see if you can find a brook or pond nearby."

Nakula did as he had been asked. From the top of a tree, he shouted out excitedly, "I see a small lake to the north. The water looks clear and fresh. It's barely half a mile away." He rushed down the tree with this information. Bhima pointed to the stag which was visible and just out of the range of Arjuna's best arrows.

A lake!

"Look! The stag is over there to the south! If we go north, we will have to abandon the hunt."

Arjuna did not want to do that. Nor did the others. Yudhishthira suggested, "Nakula! Go to the lake and fetch us water while we keep a lookout for the stag here. The stag must be thirsty too! Go quickly and return so that the stag does not get a chance to rest."

So Nakula went north to the lake while the rest of them

watched the stag which grazed quietly just out of the range of their weapons. They were too tired to chase it, but they felt that as soon as they had drunk some water they would be able to finish the hunt.

Many minutes passed. A ghati (about 24 minutes), then two by Sahadeva's estimate. The sun continued to beat down on them. The stag continued to graze. What was Nakula doing? Why did he not return? Yudhishthira then sent Sahadeva to fetch water and find out what had happened to Nakula. Sahadeva did not return either. Arjuna was next and then finally Bhima went. Nobody returned. The exiled King decided to abandon the hunt. What has happened to his brothers? Were they in trouble? This was not usual.

Yudhishthira followed the track to the lake, and when he reached the lake he found his brothers lying by the side of the water. They were not breathing. He went from body to body, holding each one and feeling for a heartbeat; he listened for the sound of air

Dead?

going in and out of the nose. There was no heartbeat. They had stopped breathing. They were dead. There were no wounds visible. There were no signs of fighting or any blood. *How did they die?*

They had survived twelve years of exile together. The sorrows he had refused to acknowledge rose from the depths and grief overtook him. He spoke to them as though his voice would draw them out of this deepest of deep sleeps.

"Nakula! O, beautiful Nakula! Playful Nakula! Wake up and tell me how this trick works. For even in this strange sleep, your eyes seem to be filled with the eagerness of play! How will I explain to Kunti what has happened to you? How will I explain to Draupadi that her youngest husband, the one who chased her playing 'Tag' and 'Hide-and-seek' when we were first married, is dead?"

His words made no difference. Sahadeva, skilled with horses, lay still with one arm stretched out with his sword drawn. Arjuna was kneeling bent forward over his knees with his bow in one hand, while several arrows had fallen out of an almost empty quiver. Bhima was in the pose of a wrestler, a toppled statue with bent knees and taut hands.

THE YAKSHA

Yudhishthira looked around for an enemy who might have accomplished this but saw nobody. The water looked cool and refreshing and he was extremely thirsty. He walked to the edge and bent down to scoop up a drink when a voice boomed out, "Stop!"

Yudhishthira looked up. The sound appeared to have come from across the lake. On the other side a herd of elephants were bathing in the cool waters. To the left was a small glade and a tall sambhar deer was drinking from the lake. In the middle of the lake was a suspicious stillness that indicated the presence of gharials. A crane was perched in the middle of the lake and it was the only creature facing him.

The voice had been very loud. *Surely,* thought Yudhishthira, *these other animals would have heard it and been startled.* Maybe he had imagined it. He was still thirsty. He bent down again and this time he heard, "Stop, Yudhishthira! Do not drink my water!"

A Crane   At the very first word, Yudhishthira had stood up and looked around to see if he could locate the source of the sound. The panorama was unchanged – none of the animals had moved and none of them seemed to have heard the voice. The voice had only spoken to him. It had just claimed ownership of the water.

"Who are you?" shouted Yudhishthira. "Show yourself. You claim this water? What right do you have to make this claim?"

"You are the interloper here, Yudhishthira!" said the voice, "If you drink this water without my permission, you will die, like your brothers."

"You killed my brothers?! How is that possible? They have no wounds. They show no sign of struggle. They are unequalled in fighting skill. What magic did you use? Even the youngest, Nakula, has faced rakshasas and gandharvas, and bested them. Surely you could not have defeated them in single combat."

"I gave them the same choice that I give you. Answer my questions and I shall let you drink your fill. If you do not wish to answer my questions, you may leave unharmed. However, you may only drink the water after you answer all my questions."

"Who are you and by what right do you claim this lake? Can you show yourself or are you a spirit without body or form?" asked Yudhishthira.

From the centre of the lake, the crane spread its wings and stretched its neck out. It was larger than it had initially appeared and the gharials moved away from it in some haste. It was still a long way away. The voice still echoed across the lake. "I am a yaksha. For your benefit, I have taken the form of a crane," said the voice, "This lake was made by me and my people and it has served us well for many generations. Until your brothers came here, no human had seen this lake. I made this lake, I own it."

Yudhishthira considered this statement of the crane yaksha. The maker of a dam could legitimately claim the fruits of the lake formed behind the dam. That did not mean that the maker could stop any other being from drinking the water, for water was a necessity for life; however, the maker could require some compensation. Traditionally, the maker could selectively kill animals that came to drink water; but thinking beings, humans, could be charged a fee or be required to deliver some service for the water they drank. The demand to answer some questions was thus legitimate, but was it legitimate to require that these questions be answered before the water was drunk.

The laws that Yudhishthira knew of were human laws while this creature was a yaksha, a creature of the forest and not the city. The laws of the forest were not the laws of human towns or cities though human laws also derived from common basic laws. The yaksha's demand that questions be answered before the water was drunk was a subtle point.

He was thirsty, his body demanded water. It appeared that he would not get it until he had answered the yaksha's questions. He had questions of his own about the yaksha's demand. Getting answers to his questions would delay the quenching of his thirst. "Tell me, O Crane-Yaksha! Why did my brothers die? Did you kill them?"

"Yes, I killed them. Nakula was first. He was such a clever young boy with a legalistic turn of mind." The yaksha sounded wistful. "When I ordered him to stop, he demanded 'Who are you?' I told him 'I own the lake. You must answer my questions before

drinking'.   He replied, *'The shastras* [67]*say that I only owe
compensation after I drink your water.'* Such a clever boy – so young
to think of the rules that humans live by. He would answer my
questions after drinking the water. Then he drank the water and
the poison killed him."

"Sahadeva came here next, singing and whistling, even though
he said he was thirsty. When he saw Nakula lying there, he
became very cautious. He stopped singing. He looked around,
then ducked and crawled to Nakula and then looked around
again. He was the image of caution. He was also the only
brother who looked at me, in my crane form, and suspected that
I was the source of the voice. Then he decided not to heed me
when he saw the elephants and deer drinking and he asked, *'Did
the elephants and the deer answer your questions?'* When I kept
quiet, he said, *'You cannot enforce your claim. If you could it would
be different, but now I do not have to answer your questions first. If
you want to stop me, you should appear and stop me physically.'* Then
he drank the water and the poison killed him."

Yudhishthira hung his head. This was exactly like the twins.
War and confrontation was a game with rules. They played at
war by the rules and did not recognize when their rules did not
apply. He wondered what had happened to the older Arjuna and
Bhima? They should have known better.

The yaksha continued. "Arjuna was next and he did not waste
time issuing a challenge to whoever had killed his brothers.
When he got no answer, he went to the lake to drink water and I
challenged him. He could not locate me by sound, but he stood
erect, closed his eyes and raised his bow. Then he started
shooting at me. Shooting! At me! It was uncanny – he could not
consciously trace my voice but his arrows were falling all around
me.   Luckily, I do not have a body for he would have surely
killed me. I am sorry to say that I laughed at him. He did not
like that. It infuriated him. Then he made the same observation
that Sahadeva had made, that if the elephants and the deer were
drinking from the lake and not dying of poison, why would he?
Thinking that, he drank and he tried to get up, bow in hand, as
if to say, *'Now I will deal with you'* and then fell down and died."

---

[67] This is a generic reference to religious scriptures in Hinduism, both revealed and
reconstructed knowledge.

"Bhima was last. He, too, issued a challenge. He peered suspiciously at the surface of the water and slapped it to make sure that I wasn't hiding in it. He offered to fight to the death if that would bring a brother back to life. He hugged Nakula and Sahadeva. He too would not listen to me. *'I am a Kshatriya,'* he said. *'It is my right to take what I need when I need it. Especially, if it is necessary for me to give battle. Right now, I challenge you. If you have any sense of what is decent, you will reveal yourself.'* Then he did what your other brothers did – he got down and drank the water. When the poison started taking hold of him, he fought back. It surprised me that anybody could fight my poison – his body seemed to know what to do but it was not enough. It was slow going, but little by little my poison overpowered him. For quite some time, he crouched and tightened his muscles. He knew what was needed to prevent it from moving out of his belly, but he was not strong enough. He could not prevent it from moving down, starting at his belly. He knew that he would lose the battle when he lost control of his sexual organs and then his bowels. I could feel his mind's distress. The poison is of my substance – I took my time, first one leg then the other leg, creeping down his thighs and all the time I could feel his mind watching his body succumb. I went around his heart to take his arms. He kept fighting, but to no avail. When he had lost his arms as well, I took his jaw for he began to realize that he should call for help. I stopped his heart, leaving his consciousness for the last. That was the longest battle I've ever had and it lasted only a few sixtieths of a vighati."

"So, Yudhishthira! You asked and I answered. I killed your brothers with poison. They would not acknowledge my right to the water of this lake."

"I must drink the water," said Yudhishthira.

"Answer my questions and then you may drink."

Yudhishthira looked at the water. He went down to the edge and let his fingers trail through the water. His tongue was parched. "Just a small scoop," said a small voice inside him. He turned around and looked at the bodies of his brothers. *'My dead brothers. What was the use of living on?'* he wondered. *'Even if I win back my kingdom, without my brothers at my side, it will be like ashes. I should drink the water and join them in peaceful death, leaving this world to Duryodhana and Duhshasana and the others.'* He thought of Draupadi, who would be at the mercy of the Kauravas. He and his brothers had been unable to prevent her humiliation once – it had been his fault, but they had all vowed revenge. Now that the brothers were dead, any revenge would be left to him, if he survived. He had to survive. Drinking the water was out of the question. Now he was resolved, he was firm, he was *Yudhishthira*, "firm in battle", once again.

He looked up at the crane yaksha, who had now grown to giant proportions. "Ask your questions," he said.

THE QUESTIONS

The Yaksha's questions and Yudhishthira's answers are in the Appendix.

OF FAIRNESS AND LOYALTY

When Yudhishthira had answered all the questions of the crane-yaksha, the yaksha said he was pleased and permitted Yudhishthira to drink from the lake. He then offered him a boon – one of his brothers could be restored to life. Yudhishthira promptly asked for Nakula to be brought back to life. The yaksha was surprised. He said,

"You rely on Bhima for strength. Arjuna's bow was going to get your kingdom back. Nakula is not the greatest warrior. Are you sure you want Nakula back?"

Yudhishthira reminded the yaksha of one of his own questions – "What is the highest Law?" The answer has been translated as "non-violence," it has been translated as "un-cruelty", but can also mean "mercy" or "compassion". The highest law for a king was to be fair and compassionate. Yudhishthira had two mothers, Kunti and Madri. He was born of Kunti and it would be unfair to Madri if he chose another son of Kunti to be restored. Even if this resulted in his losing his kingdom forever, it was still the right choice to make.

The yaksha was impressed and restored all the Pandavas to life. As the Pandavas woke up, their hunger and thirst vanished and the magical waters of that lake re-invigorated them.

The Final Journey

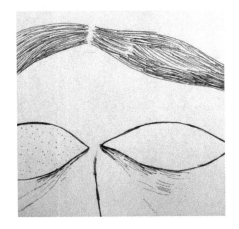

THE FINAL JOURNEY

YUDHISHTHIRA'S REFUSAL

"So be it. I will not come with you."

With these words, Yudhishthira refused to go to Heaven. Indra, the King of the Gods, had appeared with his chariot driven by six white horses and praised Yudhishthira's resolve and courage. Then he had invited Yudhishthira to climb into the chariot and come to Heaven as an honoured guest. But when Yudhishthira had made way for the dog to enter the chariot, Indra had balked.

Yudhishthira

"Chi! No, no, no. The dog is an unclean creature. It cannot come. Shush."

At these words, the dog had stopped and looked at Indra. Yudhishthira had protested.

"This dog has been my companion for this entire trip. We have come together to the top of this freezing mountain. Since Bhima fell, this dog has endured all with me – we have huddled together at night in caves, we have scrambled for a foothold on icy paths. It is a miracle that I have made it to the top. It is even more of a miracle that the dog has kept pace with me. I cannot abandon this faithful friend to freeze to death while I escape to a warm heaven. He must come with me."

Indra had been firm. "Yudhishthira, be reasonable. This is only a dog. You have been a king, a glorious one at that. What has this dog been? I can give you entrance to heaven, but on what basis would I award entrance to this dog? No, no, no! I cannot let the dog in."

Yudhishthira sighed and said, "When I proposed this path to my brothers and our wife, I did not know how it would turn out. I thought that when we reached the top of the mountain, we would get some idea of what was next, perhaps see a stairway to heaven. Bhima thought we would find the path going to the lands ruled by the pole star and going there would restore his youthful strength. Arjuna hankered after adventures like the ones we had long ago during our exile. Nakula and Sahadeva came along -- they were younger than us and did not want to come; when it became clear that we were serious, they thought we would need help. Maybe they came because we had always stayed together. Draupadi, born of fire, did not want to be subjected to the cold, but she refused to accept our suggestion that she stay behind."

He continued, "They followed me but one by one they gave up and died. This dog is the only one that did not give up. You must let him stay with me."

"No," said Indra. "You know better than that. I cannot let an unclean dog, unclean even by the standards of humans on Earth, enter pristine Heaven. Come, O, great King! Put aside these mundane attachments and come to heaven, alone."

Yudhishthira sat down on a rock and rested. The dog came over to him and put its head in his lap and looked at him. Yudhishthira patted the dog. What was he to do? The dog had survived the trek. The trek up to this point had been full of problems. Would his problems be resolved if he could get the dog into heaven? Maybe some other problem would raise its head. He knew now that his brothers had not made it and he should have suspected something when the relentlessly persevering Draupadi, Yajnaseni *born of fire*, their queen, had died on the first day. He had accepted her death on the slopes with equanimity. It had been a judgment, and he had agreed that it was the right judgment and the only possible one. And now there was only one judgment to the problem of the dog.

The dog

He looked down and across the path he had come. The last thirty or forty yards had been a pretty steep climb over rock and ice. A ridge hid the rest of the path. The mountain top that he was on was not the highest peak – on each side, a higher peak was visible and dominated. There was nothing about the path that indicated that this peak was significant in any way. There had been no signs, nor for that matter, had there been stories told by the villagers below. But here he was, being offered a ride to heaven by Indra, the king of the gods.

The panoramic view was stunning – gleaming white snow-covered peaks visible at every distance in every direction. The sky, blue as it ever could be. The sun, bright, cold, and impossible to look at, inched towards its high for the day. Far down in the valley he could see spots that could be villages, like the one that they, all of them, his wife and his brothers, had left just a few days ago. The memory of those last few days brought a frog to his throat, for he had watched them fall one by one. The memories started with the last time they had been seen in public together.

THE CLIMB

The Pandavas and Draupadi left the last inhabited village on the hillside and climbed up the snow line. They ate sparsely of the breakfast the villagers offered them, for the village was glaringly poor. They were carrying the food they had brought with them. Bhima complained that they should have brought more food, for he would have carried it. What if they did not make it to the top in three days as they had been assured by the village guide. Arjuna made fun of Bhima, saying that with Bhima's increased appetite, the greater quantity of food might last fewer days. Nakula mumbled about a breed of horse that had a thick coat and could survive under snow and ice. Sahadeva wanted to talk about the people they might meet in the lands to the north. Draupadi shushed them and told them to stop complaining like little boys. A dog followed them barking loudly until Bhima looked at it and growled. Then it yelped in fear and its tail went between its legs. Bhima laughed. Yudhishthira intervened and beckoned to the dog – it came to him and he rubbed its head. The dog stuck close to him and started following him.

When they stopped for lunch, Yudhishthira checked the pack he was carrying. He was startled to see four dice. He recognized them – with these dice he had lost a kingdom. He had kept them all these years as a talisman and reminder. He looked up and saw Draupadi smiling at him.

That was disconcerting. He had kept the dice all these years. He had played with these dice and lost his kingdom, his brothers, himself, and finally, Draupadi, to Shakuni. After that game was nullified by his uncle, he had played again and lost, with exile as the stake. Later, he had studied gambling; the great war itself had been a gamble, but never again had he gambled with dice for such great stakes. For the thirty-six years that he had ruled, he had kept these with him to remind him of his limitations. Just weeks earlier he had handed the kingdom over to his grand-nephew Parikshit and he thought he had left the dice behind.

Draupadi had suffered because of these dice. These dice had engineered her anger. These dice had been the source of her perseverance in seeking revenge. She had won, at a terrible cost. Her father had been killed, then her brother died. Her children had all died that final terrible night when the treacherous Aswatthama had set fire to the camp. She had won revenge, her husbands the instruments of her victory. Draupadi's smile was a chain linking him to this victorious past, a past that had been driven by Draupadi.

That was the last meal that they ate together as a family. It was comfortable, like the old days when they had been in exile in the forests. They were much older, but they easily settled into the camaraderie of that earlier time. But Yudhishthira was uneasy – this settling down into the dead habits of a past life was not why they had handed their kingdom over to the young Parikshit.

"Get rid of the dog," counselled Draupadi. The rest of his brothers agreed with her. The dog had settled itself down next to Yudhishthira.

"Why?" asked Yudhishthira. "It isn't causing problems, is it?"

A chorus of answers.

"We have a lot of climbing to do and it might get in the way."
"

"You might neglect some precaution because the dog was in the way."

"It's a distraction."

Yudhishthira did not want to do that. But he did not want to reject his brother's advice either.

"I'll tell you what – I'll throw the dice."

They groaned, but he did it nonetheless.

"I win," he said and collected the four pieces of bone. "The dog can stay as long as it wants."

YUDHISHTHIRA JUDGES DRAUPADI

The going was not easy – the path began as a mix of snow and slush. Then it became icy and slippery. They tied a rope around their waists and Arjuna led while Draupadi brought up the rear. The cold made it hard to speak – Yudhishthira's lips stuck to each other and his voice sounded choked. As the afternoon stretched into the evening and the sun was at the edge of a western peak, Arjuna began looking for a cave that the village guide had assured them existed. The guide had even pointed it out from the village – Yudhishthira couldn't be certain, but he thought that they must be very close. Nobody spoke much and even Draupadi and Bhima who often chatted up a blue streak were not saying much as they brought up the tail of the procession.

Suddenly Draupadi screamed. It took Yudhishthira an eternity to turn in response. Even as he turned, he felt a jerk on the rope. He held onto the rope while his feet pushed into the snow seeking a firm footing. His brothers were doing the same. Bhima was struggling to maintain his footing, but beyond him Draupadi was not to be seen but the rope leading away from Bhima's hands were taut.

Draupadi

Apparently Draupadi had slipped, but she was still attached to the rope. Bhima held firm. Nakula dug the edge of his machete into the ice; Sahadeva fell and was scrabbling for a hold. Bhima settled down into a strong low stance and pulled, while the others helped. When Draupadi finally appeared, she was limp and not conscious. She had suffered multiple wounds from the fall; she was bleeding from a blow to the head.

Yudhishthira's brothers went into a flurry of action – Arjuna had just located the cave and they gently carried Draupadi into it. Yudhishthira did his part, but Bhima was still the strongest and took charge, and so Yudhishthira stayed detached. For much of his life, Draupadi had been the engine that drove him to action. Now, she was breathing raggedly and bleeding profusely. It seemed to Yudhishthira that she would not survive and he was not surprised, for a few minutes later, she stopped breathing.

His brothers had looked at each other and then they had

looked at him. The question, as always, was what next? But what was true for him was true for his brothers as well – Draupadi had been the motive force in their lives, and now, in her absence, they were looking to him, the Eldest.

He had to decide.

For 36 years, he had been King and Emperor, ruling the land they had won after defeating their cousins and the coalition they represented. There had been peace. The judgments he had been called upon to make and the decisions that he came to affected millions. But nothing he did during that time approached the intensity of the decisions and judgments that he had had to make during the war, that he had had to make during the events leading up to the war, that he had had to make during the year of living incognito, or that he had had to make during the twelve years of exile before then. Or for that matter the decision he had made to play in that game of dice with its unpredictable consequences, unpredictably terrifying consequences.

All those decisions and judgments were now coloured by Draupadi. The game of dice had changed her life from that of a pampered princess and powerful queen to a naked supplicant in a court of insulting strangers and impotent husbands. Despite successfully restoring the Pandavas' kingdom to them with her demand for justice, she had been powerless to prevent him from gambling it all away in another final game. Her resentment had built during the twelve years of exile; the humiliations of the year spent incognito as the maid-servant of the queen of a petty kingdom, subject to the whims of her mistress and her friends, the unwanted attentions of insistent suitors unused to rejection from the powerless, had done little to take the edge off. That resentment had played itself out in the efforts towards peace made before the war started as well as its conduct.

In the privacy of their innermost chambers, decisions and judgments were the domain of Draupadi.

Now he, Yudhishthira, was being called upon to decide.

They had to go on. There was no place to cremate Draupadi's body. They could not carry a body, not even with Bhima's strength. They could not bear the thought of dragging it down or rolling it down. Nor could throw the body off the cliff and retrieve it later when they returned. But what if a wild animal found her body first – Sahadeva had turned as pale as Arjuna at the suggestion. Arjuna suggested that they could wrap her in her garments and leave her in the cave. Nakula had pointed out that the body would freeze in the cave preserving her beauty forever. There were no wild animals there to disturb her rest. Arjuna carried her to the far end of the cave and put her down in a natural sleeping pose. They made and ate their dinner in her presence, and then, unable to talk about what had happened, they made their beds and fell asleep. The dog rubbed its head against Yudhishthira's hands and then settled down.

Whatever decisions had to be made, he made.

That night, Yudhishthira dreamt. Draupadi was laughing and chatting in the company of his brothers. Yudhishthira joined them, but then everybody fell silent. Yudhishthira was hurt. "Why did you stop when I joined," he asked. His brothers glanced at each other and then finally, as always, they all looked to Draupadi.

"We have always gone on our journeys together from the very first when Arjuna won me at my father's competition. We enjoyed life together and we suffered exile together. Why did I have to die just as we started out on this final journey?"

Yudhishthira realized with a start that this was indeed their final journey. And, yes, they had set out on this journey together, as they always had in the past. But this journey, Yudhishthira realized, was not to be like the rest. Though they had set out together, they were indeed on separate journeys and their journeys could well have separate endings.

He would be called upon to make not just decisions, but also the judgments that they had so often left to Draupadi to make. Now, in this dream, Draupadi was asking for his judgment. In judgment, there could be no room for compassion. Judgment, like a persistent watch-dog, would not let go until the truth was told.

"You married all five of us but in your heart, you always favoured Arjuna."

Desert sand coated the inside of his mouth. Dry and desiccated, it choked him. Draupadi's preference for Arjuna was one of the many things that the brothers glossed over. They made jokes about Arjuna's success with women, his abduction of Krishna's sister, how he had been kidnapped by Ulupi, the Naga girl, and so on. But he had also won Draupadi and he was the one around whose neck she had first placed the victor's wedding garland. She had not married the five by her choice, but to fulfil the throwaway command of her mother-in-law that the five share equally all the gifts they received that day. But marriage was not merely a matter of wilful choice, but a sacred commitment. Once made, they should have been equal in her eyes. He knew the unfairness of this test that Draupadi had been subjected to and the unfairness of his judgment. It was the unfairness of it all that gave it this particular taste. He looked around at all his brothers to see what they made of his words. Arjuna, who had been the beneficiary of so much unfairness, looked away. Bhima's face was still as a statue. Was he thinking about the time Draupadi had come weeping to him and shown him the bruises inflicted by Kichaka [68] who had demanded that Draupadi, the maid-servant of his sister, come to his bed? He had confronted Kichaka in secret and killed him for that insolence, jeopardizing their anonymity. Nakula's eyes narrowed and he looked away too. He couldn't accept that Draupadi might prefer Arjuna's pale earnestness to his own classical beauty. Sahadeva shook his head as if in disagreement, and then he too looked away.

YUDHISHTHIRA JUDGES SAHADEVA

They woke the next day. Yudhishthira did not feel rested. They had a quick breakfast. Draupadi's body had developed a thin sheen of frost. She looked peaceful as she lay there. The dog sniffed her once and then came away before he could be chastised by one of the five. His brothers avoided looking at Draupadi directly, so lifelike in death, and yet so unlike her usual energetic self. Every day she would wake up before they did and prepare herself meticulously for the next day. This routine she had kept up throughout their exile. After the war, she added an extended ritual of taking care of her hair, brushing it down till it glowed and then carefully wrapping it up into a tight bun that stayed securely fastened to her head the rest of the day. Even at night they never saw her with her hair spread out, a sight they had gotten used to during the years of exile. Now, it would stay

---

[68] Phonetic: Kīcəkə; Syllabic: Key-chuck-u(h).

eternally fastened into a bun, a sign of that vengeance that she had finally achieved; not free as it had been for so many years, a token testimonial to her mad vow of revenge.

They left quickly, Arjuna leading as usual. They stopped for a late midday meal in a small sheltered alcove in the mountainside. At its deepest point was a surprise, a small *tulsi*[69] shrub that appeared to be still alive despite the cold. Sacred to Shiva, they felt it was a good omen. They were still not talking, like a troupe of monks keeping to a vow of silence. They sat down and slowly ate a small meal, Bhima occasionally making faces at the size of his portion. At one point, Yudhishthira glanced at Sahadeva who seemed to be engrossed looking out to the distant scenery. "That's unusual," he thought to himself, then continued eating and finished his meal. When he got up, Sahadeva was still looking out and had not moved. Yudhishthira went to him. "Sahu," he said, but Sahadeva did not respond. He put his hand out to his face – Sahadeva did not move. His face was still warm but when Yudhishthira pressed his hand against the face, Sahadeva's body toppled down. He was dead. A cobra crawled out from under his garments and quickly scuttled down a hole. Yudhishthira sat down, almost fell, to the ground next to Sahadeva's body while his brothers stood up in alarm at the sight of the body tumbling down from the rock.

Nakula held Sahadeva. His lips moved, asking his brother, his twin, to return to life. But of course, there was no answer. Bhima and Arjuna stared mutely. Nakula turned to Yudhishthira.

Sahadeva

"I thought we would make this trip together. First Draupadi, now Sahadeva. Why did my brother die?"

The dog whined. Yudhishthira's heart fell. Another judgment for him to make. Wasn't it enough that Sahadeva was dead?

"Yudhishthira, I want the truth. Why did Sahadeva die? He was the quietest one of us and went through the exile without complaining. He faced all troubles with equanimity. What did he lack that he should die at this point? Or, must we all die like this, individually and separately, one at a time?"

---

[69] Phonetic: tulsi; Syllabic: tulle-see. A shrub considered sacred in India.

It was the truth, Yudhishthira realized. They were not prepared for this climb. They were going to die like Draupadi and Sahadeva. He understood that Draupadi's partiality had been a chink in their unity. But why did Sahadeva go? Sahadeva's pride and joy had been the intelligence service he had established and run since the war. He had come into his own during the peace that followed the war, for he had been an indifferent warrior lucky to survive the great war.

"Sahadeva was very proud of his wisdom and his cleverness. He thought he knew all that went on in our kingdom and that this made him the most intelligent and most dangerous person. He could not let go of his pride. He could not share his accomplishments with the rest of us."

He felt his face harden with resolution as his brothers looked at him. Nobody said anything. As time passed after the great war, they had all become increasingly uncomfortable with Sahadeva's web. Nakula picked up his brother and with Arjuna and Bhima's help propped the proud, dead Sahadeva against the bush. There, he continued gazing out at the world and seeing its heart. Outside the alcove, the midday sun was bright. They covered their eyes against the glare of the snow as they continued up the mountainside.

YUDHISHTHIRA JUDGES NAKULA

Well before the sun set that evening they began looking for shelter. They had gone beyond the point where the village guide had any detailed information. He had indicated that the hillside was dotted with many small caves, but he had not been there himself, and what he knew had been told him by his father who in turn had learned it from his father.

They found a cave but when they went in, they found that the area near the entrance was craggy and uneven. The cave sloped in a bit and as they went in, they thought they could hear the tinkle of water. Suddenly they came out into a large chamber in the middle of which was a clear pool of water. The chamber was suffused with a faint but luminous light – a hole high up in the ceiling let in the evening sun. The effect was spectacular, if ghostly. Off to one side was a dry flat area and they headed for it. It looked like a site for a picnic for a small family.

Nakula went to the edge of the water and looked dubiously at it. There was no sign of life. He was reminded of the lake a long time ago where he and his brothers had almost died, no, *actually died*, for they had drunk forbidden water. He put in his finger and would have tasted it, except that at the last second, he balked. Instead, he used it to fix an errant hair on his moustache. The memory of the lake where they had died once was strong. He then looked at his reflection in the water.

Meanwhile, the dog came up and started lapping the water. Nakula reached over to stop it, but was too late. "It feels like that lake, doesn't it?" Bhima said and then laughed as though the laughter would dispel his unease. They all watched the dog to see what would happen to it. The dog finished drinking and then came up to Yudhishthira and rubbed against him. Nakula looked to his eldest brother who grimaced and shook his head. They all sat down to wait and see how the dog did. Yudhishthira rubbed the dog's head, and the dog wagged its tail and made a rumbling noise in its throat. After a few minutes, the dog seemed no worse off and they all looked at each other and smiled – maybe this water was not forbidden. In any case, there was no voice to warn them off.

They fetched their water bags and returned to the pool. Nakula looked at his reflection. Arjuna grumbled with good humor, "Don't worry Nakula, you haven't become old yet" and touched the surface of the water so that the ripples made it useless as a mirror. Having filled their bags, they returned to the flat area and ate a peaceful dinner. The cave felt warm compared to the place they had slept in yesterday and It was a relief to be able to speak without the effort of separating frozen lips. There was a slight draft but the wind did not howl against the mountain side.

They slept well. When they woke up the next morning, they felt cheerful. There was no light coming from the ceiling, but there was sunlight from the cave mouth which faced east. Even Bhima, who complained about the small quantity of food they had brought with them did not complain as they took a ritual bite. Nakula picked up his water-bag and drank some of the water he had filled in it the previous night. Suddenly he gagged. As they watched him, he bent over and it appeared that he was trying to spit something out. Suddenly he sagged and in the faint light all they could make out was that his face had lost its colour.

Nakula

Bhima rushed to him and held him up and slapped his back. When that failed to make a difference, he clamped his hand on Nakula's jaw and opened his mouth. A small toad looking a bit squished hopped out. Bhima grabbed at it and held it and peered closely at it. A few seconds later he shouted and dropped the toad. There was a burn mark on his hand where the toad had excreted some liquid through its skin. Nakula was still doubled over and his face had turned a dark shade. First his head, then his arms, and then his legs shuddered and twitched. Arjuna tried pouring some water on his face and then into his throat, but there was nothing to be done and they watched him stop twitching, become still and die.

The dog came up to the body and sniffed. Then it moaned as if it understood what had happened. Bhima looked at Yudhishthira and demanded, "Why did Nakula have to go? He was fair and just in all his dealings; he listened to us, his older brothers; he obeyed you unquestioningly in all things; he loved his family; he was beautiful like a god, surely the gods would have welcomed him into their midst! Why did he die and why in this hideous and terrifying manner?"

The morning cheer had abandoned Yudhishthira with Nakula's death. Why indeed had Nakula died? He had been the youngest at heart of all the Pandavas. After the horror of the war, he had been the first to recover his spirits and begin to enjoy the wealth and power that they had achieved. His older brothers had looked on indulgently as he entered a life of pleasure after the privations of exile. Nobody had felt much empathy for Sahadeva's preoccupation with secret enemies in the kingdom, and though they did not feel impelled to participate in Nakula's pursuit of pleasure, they felt they understood it.

Yudhishthira said, "Nakula thought we were wasting our time reliving our suffering during exile. He thought that he was beautiful and the rest of us were not. He thought that was the reason why we did not choose to follow his path. He was beginning to despise us in his heart."

Arjuna was startled by Yudhishthira assessment. Arjuna too had felt that they should not relive their suffering. But he had dealt with this by leaving Hastinapura on adventures. These adventures, as much as anything else, had drawn Draupadi to him. And the frequent amorous entanglements that these journeys had entailed had served to keep her just sufficiently jealous. It came to him as a surprise that Nakula had felt the way he did and chosen a different path. However, his way had given him many opportunities to exercise his martial skills and to show, repeatedly, that he had deserved to lead the Pandava army during the war. Had Nakula really thought that his adventures were an attempt to recreate the suffering of the period before the war?

Bhima was startled by Yudhishthira's assessment. The thirty-six years of peace that followed the war had been tiresome for Bhima. There had been a brief period of exhilaration when they celebrated the Ashvamedha yagna, the ritual of the Horse Sacrifice. For a whole year prior to the start of the ritual, Arjuna and he had followed the sacred horse, fighting all would-be challengers to Yudhishthira's hegemony and some others besides. That had been fun. There was a limit to the wrestling, boxing, eating, and cooking that could be done. But later, there were no feuds, no battles, nothing to compare to the war. Even the challenges occasioned by the stories of his cheating during the duel with Duryodhana had stopped. He had even spent some time in the company of Nakula's friends and had felt awkward and out-of-place in the company of the fashionable set. He had even considered challenging Yudhishthira for the kingship, but Yudhishthira then told him that he, Yudhishthira, would abdicate in Bhima's favour if that came about. As he grew older, he had withdrawn naturally from some of the more extreme challenges of the physical fitness groups, but the role of elder statesman fit him like an unbalanced mace.

Yudhishthira was startled by what he said too. The thought that Nakula's behaviour was driven by the desire not to relive the exile was not new, but that Nakula thought that the rest of them wanted to relive their sufferings was a revelation. "Was it true?" he wondered. This trip that now seemed to be a reprise of those hard times was not entirely his idea. A few months earlier when the Pandavas had discussed retiring to the forest, Krishna had suggested that they make this trip and had given them the directions. When news of Krishna's untimely death reached them, it had seemed an opportune time to make the change. Yudhishthira was not conscious of any wish to suffer. But then, he recalled, that Nakula had not seemed as enthusiastic as the rest but they had all assumed that they would stay together and possibly Nakula had simply given in to the flow.

YUDHISHTHIRA JUDGES ARJUNA

After laying Nakula's body out in the cave, the three of them continued up the mountain, but all conversation had come to an end. The dog stayed close to Yudhishthira. They seemed to need more rest stops and it seemed to Yudhishthira that the dog was more eager to continue this trek than Arjuna or Bhima. They ate when they felt like it, without coordinating with each other. Late in the afternoon, well before sunset, they came to a cave. Arjuna stopped and said, "We should stop for the night here."

Yudhishthira was surprised. It seemed to him that it was still a few hours to sunset and the peak to which they were headed seemed to be close by. "Let us keep going," he said, "We can make it to the top today."

"No. I want to stop now. We can reach your goal tomorrow." Arjuna could not keep the anger and resentment out of his voice.

After they had left Hastinapura, they had first passed by the red lake where Arjuna had received the gift of his bow, the *Gandiva*[70], and its inexhaustible quiver. There they had been accosted by an invisible voice that had demanded that Arjuna throw the bow into the lake. Arjuna had not wished to do so, for no conditions had been laid on him when the bow was gifted to him. But the voice had insisted and when Arjuna had tried to return to the path with the bow, the trees on either side of him had burst into flame and driven him back to the lake's edge. This time when the voice repeated the demand, his brothers had echoed it and Yudhishthira had counselled Arjuna not to be attached to the bow. Reluctantly, Arjuna had cast the bow and the quiver into the lake and watched as an invisible current drew the bow and quiver into the distance until they could not be seen. The voice did not come again and Arjuna's movements were not hindered anymore.

Arjuna had grumbled that they should have found and fought the spirit or yaksha that had forced him to return the Gandiva,

---

[70] Phonetic: Gāndīvə; Syllabic: Garn-dee-vu(h). The name of Arjuna's bow, a gift from the gods. Possibly means "tough as a rhinoceros".

but Yudhishthira had pointed out that they had retired from kingship and war. Now they were dying one by one and Arjuna felt that Yudhishthira did not care. Yudhishthira had shown no emotion when their queen Draupadi had died; instead he seemed to think that she was partial to Arjuna. Then he had accused Sahadeva of pride in his power over people through intelligence and Nakula of pride in his beauty. If a Kshatriya could not take pride in physical and mental expressions of power, what could they be proud of? He, Arjuna, was the best bowman there was and had ever been, and he had been forced to relinquish his celestial bow, his pride and joy!

Arjuna put down his bag and turned to face Yudhishthira. He glared at his brother, his hand moved up to his chest, he grimaced, and toppled forward. Bhima stepped forward and held him, but Arjuna was limp. He laid him down and turned him over. He was dead.

Arjuna

Bhima turned to Yudhishthira, anger and accusation in his eyes. His voice came out cracked and hoarse. "Oh, wise elder, what were Arjuna's faults that he died now within sight of the goal? He was the bravest of us, leading the army without slacking throughout the war; he endured the most beginning with that day when he was called on to share the wife he had won; he kept his vows including the ones made in the heat of battle or the rush of anger; he was most obedient to our mother's commands and to your commands; he was most in control of his attachments; he brought the great Krishna to our side without which we would have certainly lost."

The dog sat next to Arjuna's body and howled. Arjuna had barely paid attention to it and its howl made Bhima's hair stand on end. He found himself getting irritated at the dog. He kicked ineffectually in the direction of the dog and it walked casually back to Yudhishthira.

Bhima had been the closest to Arjuna and shared with him his attitude to war. He too had gone on adventures, though not as many as Arjuna, nor was he as successful in love. Yudhishthira had kept him from departing on adventures – he was the designated crown prince and could not be as free as Arjuna. He had relished Arjuna's stories on his return, keeping his envy in check. He had even restrained himself when Yudhishthira responded unemotionally when the twins died. But now, with Arjuna gone, he confronted Yudhishthira angrily.

Yudhishthira stood still, unmoving. The wind died. The world stopped. Yudhishthira said, "Arjuna was proud of his skill with the bow and with his heroism in battle. He boasted that he would defeat all our enemies single-handedly, something he could not accomplish. He was jealous of anybody who might be a better archer and he acted to ensure that a rival did not appear. He was attached to is bow Gandiva that had been gifted to him for the war and did not yield it until forced to do so. This death was the fruit of his attachment."

Bhima was not satisfied. "You have glib answers to all these questions. There are just the two of us left. Will I be next? Or will it be you? Perfect that you are, it must be me. What are my faults for which I will die next? Death will be a relief after watching my brothers go in this fashion."

Yudhishthira did not move. His tone was unchanged. He said, "Bhima, I have loved you and all our brothers since we were children and capable of love and loyalty. I have loved Draupadi as much as any of you. She was our queen and rightfully so. Sahadeva did what he had to for us, all of us. But what he thought about, whether about his actions or about himself, produced its fruits. Nakula fought in a war despite despising all that the war made him do. It had been an ugly war. The twelve years of exile to uncivilised forest had been excruciatingly painful. After the war he wanted to enjoy the things he had missed – music, dance, drama, discussions with the knowledgeable experts. He was proud of his accomplishments; he felt he knew more than his brothers. His death was the result of overweening pride. Arjuna could not exert himself fully until Bhishma and Kutaja were dead – he loved his enemies too much. Then, even after Abhimanyu's death, it took an extreme vow for him to kill the foolish Jayadratha. Only after Kutaja died did Arjuna exert himself and force the final battle with Karna that helped end the war in short order. His capacity for love and affection was great but so was his need for love. These desires affected him. You, too, have a large heart. But that great heart came with other great excesses. Hunger makes you blind to the needs of others. When you eat, Wolf-bellied one, you pay no heed to those around you, whether elder or younger, whether poor or rich, whether hungry or satiated. In the heat of anger, you vowed to kill all our cousins in war and you did. That was a vow that a Kshatriya could be proud to have satisfied. But, continuing in that heat of anger, you vowed to drink Duhshasana's blood – such a vow did not merit fulfilment, but you chose to fulfil it. Again, in that same heat, you vowed to break Suyodhana's thighs. You could have fought him in a lawful manner, but you chose to fulfil your vow and break his thighs in a mace duel – that action was illegitimate. In the heat of the moment, your self is all you see."

It had been a long speech after many days of quiet. Yudhishthira turned his back on the shocked Bhima. He looked up at the peak. It would be possible to reach it today but there was no hurry. He was not hungry, so he sat down with the dog and fed it the few scraps that he had left. He then lay down in a corner of the cave and fell asleep.

The dazed Bhima held Arjuna in his arms and cradled him. Tears flowed, for his brothers, for his wife, and for himself. Tears flowed for the sons Abhimanyu and Ghatotkacha, killed in the war in which the Pandavas had sought revenge for Draupadi. Tears flowed for the teachers and the elders, the friends and the enemies, the high and the low, all killed so many years ago, so wastefully in a war nobody needed but all desired.

A MAN AND HIS DOG

In the morning when Yudhishthira woke up, Bhima too was dead, Arjuna in his arms. The dog sniffed and moaned. Yudhishthira felt hungry. It would take a few hours to reach the summit and he would need his strength. He looked through Bhima's and Arjuna's bags and ate some breakfast. He fed the dog. He put together a bag of food that might be needed to reach the peak and set off for the summit.

Bhima

He felt faintly relieved. Judgments and decisions. They had been so easy to make as a young prince and when they had first returned to Hastinapura with Draupadi in tow. Then the disastrous dice game in which he had repeatedly made the wrong call, lost his brothers, lost himself, and then wagered Draupadi, their wife-in-common and lost. Moved by Draupadi's impassioned outburst, their uncle Dhritarashtra had done the right thing – she had saved them, letting them escape Shakuni's clutches. Then invited to play one last throw, he had done it again – he had agreed to it, despite all the advice and lost the kingdom. This time she could not do anything and they had had to go into exile. After the Great War, he had been surrounded by advisors, ministers, and others eager to provide reasons for decisions and eager to please their king. Draupadi, Sahadeva, and Nakula had happily taken charge of various aspects of a peaceful reign; Arjuna and Bhima had managed the army; with Krishna's support their empire had survived and he had not had to make unsupported judgments.

These last two days without all those accoutrements of power had been excruciatingly difficult. The words he had spoken to Bhima, that came out of his own mouth, seemed alien and distant to him. But they had indeed come from him and they mirrored his thoughts. He was at a loss to explain why he thought this and not something else. The fabric of reality behind these judgments seemed to be coming apart. He had said that Bhima was blind to the needs of others when he ate. But he could not recall a single instance of observing Bhima eat. Did he keep his mouth closed? He could not remember. He was sure he was right that Bhima had been insensitive when hungry, and he surely had observed Bhima eating often, in their very long life together. Why couldn't he recall a single image of Bhima eating? The images that had crowded his mind just a few days ago seemed to have vanished leaving these ephemeral orphaned thoughts.

He sighed and the dog sighed with him. That brought a brief grin of pleasure and he bent down and put his arms around the dog and held it. He was surprised to find that the dog was straining forward, eager to move on along the path. It acknowledged him briefly but it was as eager to go on as he felt he should, too. But what would he find at the summit? Would he be able to face it without his brothers?

JOURNEYS END?

Yudhishthira and the dog reached the summit at midday to find that it was not a sharp peak but a large flat area about the size of a temple pool. Not a big pool, but one that might be attached to a small village temple. There was nothing else there. The view was spectacular. Even though this was not the tallest summit, and there were peaks on all sides that looked down upon this one, this peak seemed to provide a particularly clean perspective on the entire world arrayed around them. The sun at the zenith of its daily path illuminated everything fiercely. There were no more secrets from this peak. Yudhishthira went to the northern edge of the summit and looked out. The dog barked suddenly and he turned around to see what it was barking at and a shining chariot had appeared behind him. Indra, the king of the gods – but who else could it be with those thousand shining eyes – looked down at him and smiled.

"Yudhishthira! Great and glorious King! I have been awaiting your arrival to give me company in heaven. Come, make haste, do not tarry here in this cold peak, splendid though it is. Enter my carriage and let me be the first to welcome you to heaven."

Yudhishthira bowed his head out of respect to the king of the gods. "Great Indra! I am indeed blessed to behold you thus. I am overwhelmed by your kindness in offering me this invitation. Surely, heaven will be sumptuous and comfortable compared to this cold summit. Surely, the sights visible from heaven would rival the splendour and beauty of the sights visible from anywhere on earth, let alone from this peak. Surely, my mind urges me to go with you, even to go ahead of you to await you in heaven. But my heart is low and filled with sorrow and foreboding. At such a time, how can I come?"

"What is it that is bothering you, Yudhishthira?"

"Sir! It has been a long journey from Hastinapura. Much has happened. The elegant Draupadi, strong inside, yet fragile for she is used to the comforts of the palace, died and her body is ensconced in a cave below. How can I go to heaven without her?"

"Yudhishthira! Your beautiful wife, whose charm and beauty rivals that of my beloved Sachi, has ascended to heaven in spirit and I know that she awaits you there. Come, let this not be a barrier to our leaving this cold place that challenge even my powers."

"Sir, I am indeed glad to hear that Panchali is not subject to the vicissitudes of a cold ice cave. But, what of my brothers whom I loved more than life itself? They have fallen by the wayside and their bodies have been pushed and stuffed in various places. I could scarcely move Arjuna and Bhima, and their bodies will soon provide fodder to whatever hungry and miserable creatures survive in this region. I cannot leave without at least attempting to bring them back. With your powers, all is possible."

Indra laughed, and the laugh echoed round the mountains. "Yudhishthira! The wise man knows not to confuse the body with the mind or the spirit. Your brothers' bodies are now merely broken vessels that leaked out the spirit upon death. Just like Draupadi, your brothers also await your coming to heaven. To you, I extend the honour of entering heaven in the body that you bore while on earth, though assuredly, you will assume a youthful raiment more suitable to the heavenly abode. Come, let us not keep in suspense the ones who wait for you."

"O, King of the gods! The news you bring is the most welcome that I have heard in many days. My hesitations are gone and I will gladly enter your chariot." With these words, Yudhishthira made his way to the chariot entrance. The dog came along and as he was about to place his foot on the lowest rung of the chariot steps, the dog jumped up and started entering the chariot.

"Shoo!" said Indra, and he tried to chase the dog out of the chariot. Yudhishthira stopped.

"Sakra! Forgive me, but the dog is my friend. He is quite tame and well-behaved. He will not hinder us during our trip. I cannot leave him alone here on this mountain top. That would be exceedingly cruel and I have compassion for him. Please allow him to travel with us."

"Yudhishthira! Your accomplishments on earth and your wisdom have attained for you a status equal to mine in heaven. You are being welcomed in the body you wore on earth. Do not make light of this offer. There is no cruelty in letting the dog stay here. He has not attained your status."

"Thousand-eyed one who sees all that is innermost in the heart! You know what is right! I too know what is right and it appears to me that this would be a monstrous wrong. I do not desire entry to a prosperity based on what I know to be unrighteous."

"There is no place in heaven for a dog. There is no place in heaven for a person with a dog. The guardians and maintainers of heaven, the *Krodhavasa*, who track the merits and demerits of the humans residing there would find you unworthy of staying in heaven in a moment. Knowing this, O Just King of the Earth, realize there is no cruelty on your part. This is the nature of the moral universe and it is just that you abandon the dog. Again, there is no cruelty in this."

"O great Indra! I have ruled on earth and not in heaven. I do not know the rules of heaven. But on earth it was my vow, one that I never abandoned, that I would never withdraw my sanctuary from one who is terrified, from one loyal to me, one who seeks my protection, nor one who is destitute, sick, weak and unable to protect oneself. This dog has done all that and more, for it has been a comfort and a solace at a time of great loss. When I lose my earthly life, I can consider releasing myself from my vow, but not before then. It would be a sin and I would not merit any heaven, and I cannot enter heaven at your invitation while committing such a sin."

Indra stepped down, put an arm around Yudhishthira and smiled. He said, "Think again, O great king! The Krodhavasa will take away all the merit accrued from gifts, sacrifices, libations to the sacred fire. I repeat, all merit is lost if a dog is a witness. This dog cannot be admitted to heaven for it would crack the very foundation of it. Abandon this dog and achieve heaven. By abandoning your brothers and the dark-skinned beauty Draupadi you have acquired dominion over a swathe of heaven that will dumb-found you with its wealth and prosperity. You have renounced everything else, why stay attached to this dog?"

Yudhishthira was unmoved. "This dog, O Sakra, is alive. When a being dies, there is neither friendship nor enmity with that dead being. When Draupadi died, and could not be revived, she was no longer a wife, a lover, or a friend; when my brothers died and could not be revived they were no longer brother, friend, or co-husband. I was right to abandon them then but I did not abandon them while they lived. But to abandon a living being that is a loyal friend is the highest sin, bar murder. I will not abandon this dog."

A man and his dog

So. There they were, on the mountain-top, Yudhishthira and the dog, sitting on a rock looking out at the scenery, the sun shining brightly down. Indra could not dissuade Yudhishthira. He stood with one foot on the ground, the other foot in the chariot. He shook his head and stepped into the chariot slowly, looking back at Yudhishthira in case he changed his mind. But there was no sign that Yudhishthira was re-considering his decision. Indra entered and sat down. Again, nothing. Finally, he waved his hand and the chariot vanished with a loud sound.

Yudhishthira looked at the dog. "Well," he said, "It's just the two of us now. I guess we have to go back down now for I cannot take care of you here."

The dog did not say anything. It looked at Yudhishthira and barked.

Heaven

Another loud crack sounded. Yudhishthira looked up to see that Indra had returned with his chariot, along with a retinue of gods. To Yudhishthira's amazement, the dog disappeared and was replaced by another god, the dark-skinned terrifying god, Dharma, and Dharma smiled at him. The gods gathered around Yudhishthira. Then Dharma said, "O great King! You have set a shining example of compassion for all creatures and justified your birth in the dynasty of Bharat. This is not the first time that I have tested you. I was the yaksha in the forests of Dwaita who took the lives of your brothers and after examining you offered you the opportunity to revive one. You chose Nakula for you wished to be fair to your step-mother, and disregarded your own need for the strength of Bhima or the skill of Arjuna. Now, to protect a loyal dog, you renounce a divine invitation to heaven. You have no equal even in heaven, O King! You have won all the rewards that heaven can bestow on you."

With these words, all the gods invited Yudhishthira to heaven. He entered the chariot and in an instant the entire assemblage was transported to the court of Indra, where all the royal sages of antiquity were seated with Narada at the head. And Narada, too, felicitated Yudhishthira, "You have achieved more than all the sages and kings assembled here, for you have come here in your own body. Come join this happy group and enjoy."

Yudhishthira looked around at the assembly and failed to see his brothers and failed to see his lovely wife Draupadi. A veil of doubt and suspicion fell over his face. He bowed deeply to all the assembled sages and the gods, and he said, "Happiness for me is to be where my brothers are. Quick, take me there for I do not see them here. This cannot be the place meant for me."

Hearing these words, Indra hastened to convince Yudhishthira with good sense, "O King! You have come here with your earthly body, and retain the attachments that pertain to humans. You have attained heaven by your great deeds, now let go of those physical limitations, and live here joyfully without those longings for your brothers and your wife."

Yudhishthira surveyed the assembly. There was smiling and laughter all around. It was a vision of Heaven. The taste of Heaven, the smell of Heaven, the cool breeze of Heaven caressing his shoulders, the beautiful and splendid sights, and the sounds of joy and laughter engulfed him. But he was conscious of a loss that these sensations did not satisfy.

Then, he saw Suyodhana.

Suyodhana was seated on a palatial couch surrounded by his friends and by sages and by other beings of great knowledge and understanding. Suyodhana was smiling, and he was laughing, and he was exulting in the taste, smell, touch, sounds, and sights of Heaven. And Suyodhana looked at him and smiled in welcome.

But where were his brothers?

He ran through the assembly while the gods and the sages looked on in amazement. He ran past Suyodhana and he saw other kings, both friends and enemies who had fallen in the Great War. He did not see his brothers. He ran and ran. Finally, exhausted, he stopped. He looked around. He was back to where he had started running. He addressed the assembly of the gods and the sages.

"How can I share joy here with this selfish and myopic Suyodhana? He was responsible for the slaughter by us of friends and relatives in retaliation for our exile to the forest. He was responsible for causing Draupadi to be dragged into the court before the family elders. I don't even want to see him, let alone share joyful company with him. Where are my brothers, I wish to go there!"

The sage Narada[71] smiled indulgently at Yudhishthira. "All enmities cease in heaven, o king! A king who sacrifices himself in battle achieves the heaven of heroes and is worshipped with the gods by those who understand this. Suyodhana indeed qualifies to be here. He did persecute you and your brothers but he observed the practices of his caste and is rightfully here."

Yudhishthira stared at Narada. *Did Narada mean what he had just heard?* Suyodhana qualified to be here despite his malevolence, despite his pettiness and despite his short-sightedness. But why were his brothers, who had been above malevolence, above pettiness and above short-sightedness not here?

Narada continued, "My son. Heaven is for forgetting. Forget the sorrows that you bore because of the dice game. Forget the sufferings of Draupadi. Forget the pain that you suffered because of war. Meet Suyodhana as a friend here, with open arms. This is heaven where enmities are forgotten."

Yudhishthira collected himself. It was true that Suyodhana had been his enemy, but if Suyodhana's actions merited him a stay in Heaven, so be it – it was not for him, Yudhishthira, to judge. But his brothers were still missing. If this region of heaven were reserved for the Suyodhanas of the world who had fulfilled their duty and died in battle as Kshatriyas, there must be other, greater regions reserved for people like his brothers, or Karna, or others who had gone beyond the mundane requirements of caste duty or who had endured more and had become stronger thereby. He replied to Narada, "I understand that these are the regions reserved for heroes like Suyodhana. Where are the regions reserved for my courageous brothers who kept their vows and were truthful in speech? Where would Karna, my elder brother, who died for my benefit, be? Where would the others like Drishtadyumna, Satyaki, and other Kshatriyas who also met their death in honourable battle be? Why don't I see them? I want to see Virata, Drupada, Drishtaketu, Shikhandin,

---

[71] Phonetic: Nārədə; Syllabic: Na(h)-ru(t)-the. Narada is a divine sage and philosopher who commiserates with the unfortunate, spreads news and gossip, and often foments conflict.

Draupadi's sons, Abhimanyu. The list is endless and I want to see them, not Suyodhana and his brothers."

NOT HEAVEN!

He turned to the rest of the gods who stood quietly listening, "Oh gods! I do not find my brothers here, nor can I find Karna, Radha's son, Yudhamanyu and Uttamaujas, and other *maharathas*, great chariot warriors, who stood by us in the war. All of them died in battle and only if they too attained this region of heaven will I stay here. If not, I shall not live here. At my mother's request, I offered water for Karna's soul and grieved when I discovered the truth about Karna, for I had wondered at the resemblance between his feet and hers; I caused him to be killed by Arjuna instead of acknowledging him as eldest. I want to see him along with Arjuna and Bhima. I want to see my wife the princess of Panchala. What is heaven to me without these people? That is the truth. This is not heaven."

On hearing this, the gods said, "Child! If that is what you desire, go there without delay." And they turned to Indra and said, "We will do as Sakra[72] commands."

Indra turned to Yudhishthira and said, "I cannot take you there myself, and nor will any of the gods. But I will ask a messenger to take you as far as he is able, to the regions that your brothers occupy." And Indra and the gods disappeared.

Yudhishthira waited. He was exhausted. The trek up the mountain-side had been hard. He had struggled to contain himself as he watched his brothers and wife die – that had been gut-wrenching. The choice he had been offered to abandon the dog had squeezed out the energy for making decisions. When the dog turned out to be a god, and he was taken to heaven to see his brothers, he had a relaxed a bit, but there had been no rest. His brothers had not been there and he was being sent on another trek of unknown length. He felt like giving up. But giving up would have meant enduring the sight of his enemy Suyodhana, who was enjoying heaven. He needed his brothers. He needed his wife. They provided the meaning for his life and that thought energized him.

---

[72] "The mighty one", one of Indra's many names. Phonetic: Śākrə; Syllabic: Sha(rp)-cru(st).

It struck him that, luckily, he did not have to take care of the dog anymore. The thought made him feel freer, but only for a moment, as he recalled that the dog had merely been a test. But what a useless test for it assumed that he wanted to be in a heaven that did not include his brothers and wife. How could the gods, including Dharma, the god of Law, engage in such a charade? Indra had claimed that because he still had his earthly body he was thinking like an earthbound being. Did that mean that the gods did not feel the earthly passions, that they felt no compassion, no joy, and no sorrow? Did a god have any feeling or sensation whatsoever? Why smile then? What difference did it make then whether heaven smelt like a lotus in full bloom or like a cesspool overflowing? Why would a god care if the denizens of earth did good or evil if they could not feel it?

THE ROAD TO HELL

The solution to this conundrum escaped him. As he stood there waiting, Indra's messenger appeared. "Follow me, o King!" he said and led Yudhishthira along a path out of the assembly. "What is the region called, that contains my brothers and wife?" asked Yudhishthira. "It has no name," said the messenger. They had reached the outer edge of an enormous field and were looking down onto the earth. Shimmering paths led in many directions. As he watched, they seemed to change, some disappearing when he tried to focus, others becoming sharp. Some of the paths seemed to be avenues lined with shady trees that would have been a pleasure to walk along. Other paths led up to a blinding place higher up. Some paths led down and he could see one winding down to the top of a mountain. There were paths that were well- lit and there were paths that were utterly dark. "What is this place called?" asked Yudhishthira. "It has no name," said his guide.

Yudhishthira pointed to a path leading down to a mountain top. "What is that path called?" he said. "It has no name," said the guide, once more.

Why did this guide not know anything about where we are going? "Where are we going?" asked Yudhishthira, a frown on his face. The guide pointed to one of the paths shrouded in darkness. "That way," he said, and he walked confidently into the darkness.

Yudhishthira followed the messenger. The messenger's golden clothing was barely visible as faint outline. There was light coming from somewhere but Yudhishthira could not make out where it was coming from. He cautiously put a foot on the path. He almost slipped for the way felt slippery. He wriggled his foot and obtained a firmer grip. He looked down and realized that he was stepping on some slime. It was pitch-black when he entered the path, the messenger's clothing providing a little fluorescence, but as his eyes adjusted he could see a little more. Not much more, for he could barely see the path that the messenger was following. The messenger seemed to have no trouble following the path, and he started with a brisk pace. Meanwhile, Yudhishthira was having a hard time keeping up – he was tired, but he was also old, and he did not have the youthful body and spring that the messenger seemed to have. The path smelled of death – a mix of bad meat, blood, and sewage – and Yudhishthira thought he saw the skeletons of various animals, a bear, a human corpse, a shadowy dog or wolf dragging something. There was a sound, a loud buzzing as of bees or wasps and occasional slurping or sucking sounds. To one side, it appeared there was a marsh and things fell into it and sank slowly while Yudhishthira watched in shock. Occasional bursts of marsh gas ignited in a blazing fire that gave light, not enough to see, but enough light to imagine, and in Yudhishthira's state he imagined the worst. Crows and vultures and other birds seemed to flit by, carrying pieces of dripping organs in their beaks. "Stop! Please go slower!" shouted Yudhishthira for it seemed that the messenger was racing on ahead oblivious as to whether he was being followed.

The messenger stopped and retraced his steps. His voice had hardened.

"You wish to return, old man?" he said.

"No," said Yudhishthira, "I can only go so fast. I cannot see as well as you. The sensations are overwhelming. You must walk slower and make sure that I am following you."

"I smell nothing," said the messenger.

"What is this place?" asked Yudhishthira, but he knew the answer before the messenger gave it.

"It has no name," said the messenger, apparently still

unconcerned by his inability to name the region it was in.

"What are these things I see faintly?" asked Yudhishthira. "My imagination carries me away and I see the most grotesque things."

"Shall I describe the scene?" said the messenger, "I can see clearly."

"Yes, please."

"You are walking on a path that was covered with moss, but the moss has been overlaid with the unburnt hair of cremated corpses. Over there is a pile of corpses from the little to-do that the Vrishnis and the Andhakas and the Bhojas[73] had a few months ago. All of your friend Krishna's relatives died in that melee. Their bodies come here. The slushy noise you hear is from a hundred thousand worms that have made their homes in those corpses. The buzz is of blood-sucking flies that have congregated here to feed on the thawing blood of those heroes. Beyond the pile of corpses, you see an iron palace set on a steep unapproachable hillside. There live a thousand ghouls and vampires, allocated to this pile of corpses; it is mid-day now so they are still inside, but at night they will come out and attack the mound. In another ten years, they will have consumed it all. You should watch your step in this place for you might trip on a hand or a foot or even a head."

Yudhishthira shivered. He recalled the last meeting he had with Krishna, at which his friend had bemoaned the meaningless slaughter that the Vrishnis and Andhakas and Bhojas had engaged in. Some of these corpses had been his friends. If he could believe Indra these corpses did not have spirits animating them. Why were they being subject to such treatment? It did not make sense.

Yudhishthira could not focus – his mind continued to race ahead seeing things that might be there. The path too changed. Whenever he felt he had just managed to get command of his stepping, the feel of the path would change. It was slimy; then it

---

[73] Krishna is a Yadava ("descendants of Yadu"). The Yadavas are organized into clans: Chedi, Vidarbha, Satvata, Andhaka, Kukura, Bhoja, Vrishni, Shainya and Haihaiya. Of these, the Vrishni, the Andhaka and the Bhoja clans figure prominently in the Mahabharata. A short time before the Pandavas went on this journey the Yadavas killed each other in a civil way and Krishna died.

was treacherous with objects that might be tree limbs or human organs; then it appeared that he was walking alongside a river of boiling water that overflowed its banks and he had to step gingerly, for his feet could be burnt. He could not believe that this was the way to the place that his brothers were in and he wondered if the messenger was lost.

"Are you sure this is the way?"

The messenger speeded up. "Yes," he said.

Yudhishthira said, "You don't seem to know where it is we are going. Whenever I ask you for the name of the region, you say it has no name."

"That is true," said the messenger. "This is heaven. In heaven, things are not named. I know the way to where your brothers are, but it is not a place with a name. And the way will be different tomorrow, for there is no one way to anywhere. Do not step off the path for you will not step back onto the path that I follow."

Yudhishthira absorbed this new piece of information. He was not being offered a choice, he just would have to be patient. A tree-branch with a few dried leaves on it was hanging across the path. Absent-mindedly, Yudhishthira used his left hand to push it to one side and as he did it, he heard a hoarse laugh and the branch whipped away. His arm throbbed with pain from palm to elbow and there was a bloody slash all along his arm. The pain was like fire, he wanted to run to the boiling water of the river, but he held himself back – he was a Kshatriya and he could take this pain. In the dim light, he could not make out what was happening but there must have been some poison in the leaves for his arm swelled and a foul odour came from it.

"Be careful what you touch," said the messenger. "The leaves in this forest are made of sharp iron knives and swords abandoned by warriors in battle."

That advice is a little late! thought Yudhishthira.

As Yudhishthira continued behind the messenger, he saw a wide expanse of sand glowing red like the iron sands of Jambudvipa's Southern Ocean. Faintly he could make out men, or at least creatures on two legs, driving horses or donkeys. Tied to each animal were ropes from a hundred other men and women who seemed to be dancing. He heard shouts of "Please slow down! Oh! My feet are burning! Please, sir!" but the drivers were oblivious to these requests.

"Messenger! What is going on there?"

"Those are the liars and cheaters on earth who are being driven across blazing sands to atone for their lies."

Suddenly a rock came flying from the procession of liars and landed right in front of Yudhishthira. "Watch out," said the messenger, but it was too late. Yudhishthira stepped on the rock. The rock was hot and Yudhishthira hopped off it but now he had a large blister on his right foot. He stopped and swatted at the ember to get it out. The blister grew bigger. When it stopped swelling, he pricked it with a nail and watched it drain. It still hurt to walk on it. He tried hopping on the left foot, but that did not work well. After a few hops, he tried limping gingerly, wincing at every step. The messenger waited while Yudhishthira limped up to him.

The messenger said, "You should be more careful – this is a very dangerous place. Do you want to continue or should I take you back?"

Yudhishthira said, "How soon will we get there?"

"This is heaven," said the messenger. "There is no time here. You will know when you get there. The journey will take as much time as it needs."

Yudhishthira shook his head. The words made no sense. They continued on their way, Yudhishthira still limping. His cut arm was bleeding but there was nothing he could do. It was also emanating a foul odour that made it difficult to breathe. The messenger did not seem to be having any trouble. Suddenly the messenger stopped.

"This is it," he said. "This is as far as I have been commanded to take you."

"I cannot see anything," said Yudhishthira. "All I sense is this repulsive smell! Are you sure my brothers are here?"

"Yes, they are here. They may be hard to find. You will have to look for them yourself."

HELL

Yudhishthira peered into the gloom. There was little to see. He felt that the messenger knew more than he was letting on, so he was not eager to step off the path. That might allow the messenger to leave and he would lose his sole hope of getting help in finding his brothers. He felt let down by Indra and Dharma – perhaps it would be better to confront them. Had they not promised him that his brothers were waiting to welcome him? How could they consider this a fulfilment of that promise? He had been lied to. If gods could lie, what could he, a mere human, do?

What should he do? Again, he was faced with this question of what judgment to make, what decisions to take, and how to execute them? In his brief glimpse of Suyodhana, he had seen him smiling and talking and laughing – he did not appear burdened with judgments and decisions. It had been so easy earlier to turn his back on Indra and decide to stay with the dog. The accepting companionship and loyalty of the dog had been compelling. But here, there seemed to be nothing to stay for and only a heaven founded on lies to turn back to.

The messenger had turned his back on Yudhishthira. "You may stay if you wish or you may return with me. Follow me, if you will." With those words, the messenger started walking and Yudhishthira noticed for the first time that the path seemed to form itself in front of the messenger, continued from the messenger to his own feet, and that a few feet behind him it dissolved. He could go back or he could step off and he had a fraction of a second to make up his mind, but that was all.

There was nothing he could do here. There were compelling reasons to return. Maybe he could remonstrate with Indra and Dharma about the way they had led him on; recount their lies and broken promises; demand that his brothers be brought up in front of him in a direct manner instead of leading him to this wasteland. He stepped on the path and started following the messenger.

All this while, there had been the hideous buzzing of the meat-eating flies and hornets. Suddenly that buzz was replaced by even more overwhelming sounds that sounded like human voices. Yudhishthira stopped and craned his head to the right side of the path to listen. "O great king! Please stay a moment."

"O son of Pandu! You brought a delightful breeze with you and it leaves with you. Stay!" "O son of Dharma! Your presence has been a great relief!" "O wise king! Seeing you has brought us great joy".

The voices recalled memories close to his heart. Each sentence was drawn out as if the speaker was in great pain. He could not make out any of the speakers and he struggled to understand what was being said. Suddenly a similar chorus rose from the left. "O son of Prtha, stay just a while longer so that we may enjoy the happiness that has come with your presence." "Please stay here, o son of Bharata!" "O Kaurava! As long as you are here, the torments do not afflict us."

Overwhelmed by these painful lamentations, Yudhishthira froze. If he had felt unable to act before, now the feeling of helplessness rose like bile and singed his throat. Tears flowed from his eyes as the voices continued, pleading for his continued stay. Some of the voices sounded familiar. He tried to focus on one of the voices but it was hard for each familiar voice was drowned out by another familiar voice. He was unable to recognize a single one in all the cacophony. Finally, when his throat began to unfreeze, he said "Who are you? Why do you stay here?"

The voices rose in volume as the answers came from all sides. "I am Karna!" "I am Bhīma", "Arjuna!" "Nakula!" "Sahadeva!" "Draupadi!" "Drishtadyumna!" "We are Draupadi's sons, killed in the fire!" Many other voices also replied, all warriors that had died in the great war. All the voices sounded as if the speaker was in great pain and were straining to shout.

Yudhishthira stopped, his mind whirling. His brothers, his wife, their children, other Pandava warriors here!? In this place that even the gods seemed to have forgotten. What was he to make of this? What destiny was it to be condemned to this woeful place? What sinful acts could the heroic and great-hearted Karna, the young sons of Draupadi, and Draupadi herself, have committed? It did not make sense that these people could have angered the gods. In any case, the gods were only in charge of heaven, they could not punish or reward arbitrarily. Or was that belief a false one? Consider that Suyodhana, with his evil mind and wicked followers appeared to be enjoying prosperity in this heaven. He was feted like an Indra, he had an adoring band of followers around him, he was smiling and drinking and laughing and had even greeted him like a fellow king. What had Suyodhana done to merit this? Considering that his brothers and his wife and their followers were generous, honest, and loyal; considering that they revered the revealed truth of the Vedas; considering that they had steadfastly acted as Kshatriyas; considering that they had performed the necessary rituals and sacrifices suitable to the gods and the ancestors – why were they here?

He recalled the story that Bhishma had told him many years ago of the sage Markandeya who had been sucked into the open nostril of a sleeping Vishnu and in an instant experienced a thousand suns and earths being formed and being destroyed, suffered through a hundred thousand lives, and then found himself expelled in the next breath of that sleeping Vishnu. Were those hundred thousand lives real or a dream? The question was not answerable. Was he suffering through a dream? It would be such a relief if he woke up and found that he was still in the palace in Hastinapura and that this had all been a dream. But that did not seem likely. Maybe he had fallen on the mountain path like his brothers and this was a nightmare he was experiencing as he lay dying on the cold summit. Maybe he had suffered an accident or an illness and these were delusions created by a diseased brain.

Unfortunately, none of these speculations helped him. If it was a dream, it was a remarkably solid one and showed no sign of going away. If he was dying on a cold hillside, he could do nothing about the illusions conjured up by his waning brain. If he was sick and delusional, it would last until he became well and, again, there was nothing to be done about it.

Except for the pain that the voices aroused in him. The aftermath of the great war had felt like this. All those dead old warriors and dead young warriors and dead children pretending to be warriors. The grieving women. He had been responsible then. But here, the voices were pleading for him to stay, for they claimed it brought a little relief from their pain. He did not have to do anything.

He just could not tell the messenger, "Take me back!"

How was he to confront the gods if he could not leave this place? And if he left this place why would he return? Already an ember of that disloyal thought was burning its way into his heart. He recalled that after the great war was over and he entered the city in triumph he had done nothing to stop the peace-loving citizens who proved their loyalty by burning the loud-mouthed Charvaka who questioned the legitimacy of his victory. That ember still stung. But, this was different, wasn't it? Whatever the sins that these beings had committed, he had not been contaminated and he could enjoy heaven to its fullest.

The memory of Charvaka whom he had failed to protect settled his mind – he could not abandon these beings that called out to him in the voices of his loved ones even if they were false. And if they were true, he needed to direct his anger towards the gods, specifically Dharma, whose realm it was to judge souls and dispose of them. His stomach grumbled and he realized that he was hungry; the foul odours of the place did not kill the appetite of his body but the combination of hunger and revulsion made him increasingly irritable. His anger mounted, and he turned furiously to the messenger. The messenger stepped back when confronted by the look in Yudhishthira's eyes.

"You! Go back to the beings who command you. Tell them that I reject their invitation and shall not return to where they are. I shall stay here. I shall stay here, and nowhere else, for my companionship comforts the ones who are bound here. If by some chance, these are truly my brothers, I would rather comfort them, than live with the lies of your masters."

Having said this, Yudhishthira sat down on the path and composed himself. He was certain that he would stay here for a long time. He sent the messenger back to Indra, the chief of the gods, and Dharma, the lord of judgment.

THE JUDGMENT OF YUDHISHTHIRA

It is said that there is no time in Heaven. Even as the messenger left and Yudhishthira sat down, the gods assembled around the seated Yudhishthira and with their arrival, the place was transformed. The foul smells were replaced by sweet ones, the buzzing sounds were silenced. The sky turned a glorious blue and light suffused the region that had once been a dark, miasmic slice of hell. The boiling river disappeared, the thorn trees were replaced with pleasant groves of mango and other fruit; the corpses that littered the land and fouled the air with the rotting smell also vanished; a gentle cooling breeze rose that carried the smell of a *saugandhika* flower in full bloom. His arm and foot stopped hurting and there was no sign of a wound when he looked at them. It was as though there had been nothing fearful or foul there.

Yudhishthira looked on in amazement at the gods gathered on all sides of him. Had they pulled him back from where he had decided to stay? Were they over-riding his decision? He stood up and prepared to address them angrily for the change was not one he was prepared to accept. Indra interrupted him.

"Yudhishthira, O great king! All these illusions are now ended. You have succeeded and passed the final test. Forgive me that you had to endure hell, but also permit me to explain why."

Yudhishthira looked at him uncomprehendingly. This was *another* test? What kind of test was it if his brothers and wife and other loved ones had to endure pain so that he could be tested? No, Indra had said that it was illusion and that the illusion was over. The messenger had not taken him to his brothers and wife after all. It had been another lie, another promise from a divinity unaccountable to anyone.

Indra continued without letting Yudhishthira put words around the growing anger, "Yudhishthira, your anger would burn heaven, do not yield to it. You are a great king and are due a great reward for your acts. But just as a king may enjoy the rewards of his good actions, he must behold hell and endure it for his bad actions. As a king, you have necessarily done both good and bad actions – for each you have earned a proportionate share of heaven and hell. If a king enjoys heaven first, he must endure hell after that. If a king endures hell first, he shall enjoy heaven later. If the sins of the king are many and good deeds few, he shall enjoy heaven first. If the sins of the king are few and good deeds many, he will have to endure hell first. I deceived you, O Yudhishthira, so that you had to endure hell first for the two sins you committed. As you deceived your guru Kutaja in the matter of his beloved son Ashvatthama, so were you led to believe that your loved ones were suffering the pangs of hell. As you permitted the harmless Charvaka to be burnt to death, so did a stray ember burn your feet, a thorn-tree branch scratched your arm and poisoned it. That being the extent of your sins, your time in hell is over. In addition, by passing this additional test, you have established your reputation as the greatest of kings. We had to deal similarly with Bhima, Arjuna, and even Draupadi for they also merited a short stay in hell. It has been many years since the war and all the kings who helped you have attained heaven. They await you! Come, my son, Yudhishthira!"

Between Indra and the other gods, Yudhishthira was pacified and re-united with his brothers, including Karna. He met everybody he knew on earth, both friends and enemies. He bathed in the Ganga as it flowed through heaven and discarded his physical body, though as with all things in heaven, it too was now eternal and he could access it if he wished. His doubts and his anger were quenched and all was well.

THE BEGINNING

But was it? For Vyaasa's Mahabharata draws a discreet curtain over further events in *Swarga*[74]. The conundrum for Yudhishthira, as it would be for anyone subjected to the whims of the gods, is how to know if any new milieu is illusion or reality. In this heaven through which Yudhishthira travels, it appears that all is illusion! But that is what our sages assure us is true of the earth. It appears, though, as if the creators of illusion in heaven have even less compunction about revealing their role – there is no man behind the curtain. Rather, there is a man alright but there is no curtain and no need for a curtain!

Look at it this way – in *Swarga*, the Vedic Heaven, all is real. Real things cannot be named – that is why nothing has a name in the heaven of this story and every path forms as one follows/discovers it. What is a name? A name attempts to represent a material object (the "real thing") symbolically; like all representations, is less than the real thing. A thing that has a

---

[74] I've used the words "Heaven" and "Hell", but those are concepts from the Abrahamic religions of the West and do not adequately represent the concept of *Swarga*. Illusion is primary in Hinduism, the heavens and hells as illusory as Earth. The illusion of Earth includes time and space, the illusion of Swarga does not. The illusion of Earth includes the belief that things exist in time and have a place in space; the illusion of Swarga is that real things have neither time nor space. Our language is barely adequate to represent things of the Earth; it is definitely inadequate to describe Swarga.

name that completely represents it cannot be real.[75] A path that is already known must be between named things and therefore cannot itself be more real than its end points.

On Earth, we *give* names to things, thus creating symbolic objects that are less than real for communicating with each other. The result is that our mental lives are lived in an unreal world of named objects that is a shadow of the real world of un-nameable objects. This does not happen in the heaven that Yudhishthira finds himself in. Yudhishthira, the human, does not have the intellectual apparatus to understand the Vedic Heaven. That inability is *Vyaasa's curtain*. He asks the messenger where he is going and thinks he has been taken to "hell" – the messenger tells him the truth that he cannot name anything in Swarga. He asks the messenger "what is the path to get there" – the messenger tells him the truth that he cannot name the path.

After washing in the heavenly Ganga, Yudhishthira is "cleansed of his sins" and "loses his earthly body" – then, he disappears behind Vyaasa's curtain and *we* do not have the intellectual apparatus to follow what happens to him

Nor is there Time in Swarga. We already know that there is no absolute Time on earth, only space-time, something created by the presence of material things (we call them "Mass" and "Energy"). Mass and Energy do not exist in Swarga; hence Space-time cannot exist. What is there is behind Vyaasa's curtain which makes it incomprehensible to our human intellectual apparatus.

And so, that is how the Mahabharata begins and ends. It begins with the origins of the Kurus from the reality or unreality of a mythological cosmos and it ends with Yudhishthira and his brothers dissolving into the reality or unreality of an illusory heaven, bracketing an illusory time.

---

[75] This contrasts with the concept of "real" names as believed in Western mysticism – the *name* of an object (its *real name*, not the name by which we refer to it) gives the *one-who-names* power over the object. This is the basis of magic as believed by the Gnostics and in the kabbalah and, for that matter, in Harry Potter's world.

End-Notes

END-NOTES

[1] TESTING THE PRINCES

Why is this test so important that it needs to be told? It's a vignette that illustrates why Kutaja loves Arjuna, possibly even as much as he loves his own son Ashvatthama. The test measures all the other pupils against a standard set by Arjuna and they all fail it.

Is that all? What, indeed, is a 'test'? It proves that a student has learned the material that has been taught. The teacher has done the job of teaching. But a good test is more than that.

But tests do not just measure, they cause learning.

All the princes, except Arjuna, fail the test. The Mahabharata does not say anything more about the consequences of this test. Arjuna is praised by Kutaja for his unwavering focus on the task at hand. *Arjuna is the greatest archer in the world and he proves it by passing the test* – is that what the poet wants us to take away?

On the surface, this episode illustrates the difference between the attentive student and the rest of us, the easily distracted. In many fields of endeavour, small differences in performance makes the difference between being the winner and being an also-ran. In such fields, focus is likely to be important.

What's this about causing learning?

What are the circumstances in which a test causes learning? Equally important is *Who learns?* – the one who passes the test, or, the one who fails it? Is it the *bystander*, watching? Or, perhaps, it is the person delivering the test, or maybe, it is the teacher who is the learner! The Mahabharata does not bother to elaborate on this and leaves us with its depiction of Arjuna's focus as the key to his skill.

What is the deeper meaning to this test? The Mahabharata *shows*, by subsequent events, and especially during the Great War and at its end, the other learning that this test engenders.

The poem tells us that Arjuna, who passes the test, becomes the champion bowman of his time. His success pre-figures that future status. He is applauded for acing the test. His success hides a greater failure – *he learns nothing else from the test.*

All the other students learn that they can become the best in other fields, just like Arjuna. He is already an expert archer. Over time he becomes a better archer. An expert is focused on achieving a simply defined goal in a domain of expertise. Archery is Arjuna's domain and he wins – his expertise will fail him later when he is faced, not with an archery contest, but with the problem of winning the war. Arjuna never delivers on his boastful claim that he would win the war single-handedly. The real war depicted in the epic is a messy affair[76].

The stories of Karna and Ekalavya highlight another aspect of Arjuna's expertise. Karna and Ekalavya are potential competitors. Arjuna has passed every test in his life with flying colours. Many students who have always succeeded and have become used to easy success are occasionally unable to handle messy, real-life problems. Arjuna must have known that confronting Karna or Ekalavya would have been true tests of skill for which he was not prepared. He then manipulates Kutaja's love for him and, as a result, Ekalavya is disabled. Kutaja refuses to teach Karna the brahma-*astra* that he may have been qualified to receive – Karna subsequently made unwise choices that led to his defeat by Arjuna.

[2] Kutaja/Drona

The earlier story, "The Education of the Princes", is the story of how Kutaja, the martial arts teacher of the Pandavas and the Kauravas, came to be a mortal enemy of Drupada, the father-in-law of the Pandavas. Drupada's rude behaviour towards Kutaja, his childhood friend, creates bad blood; Kutaja's injured pride leads him to ask his pupils to bring him Drupada as a prisoner. Drupada swallows his pride and apologizes; in return, he receives the southern half of his kingdom along with his freedom as a "gift"; Kutaja then proclaimed that as they were now equals, they could be friends; Drupada agrees and returns to his city. For the rest of his life Drupada looks for ways to get revenge.

---

[76] In the Great War, Arjuna will kill Bhishma by hiding behind Shikhandin (Amba reborn); he will kill the Sindhu king Jayadratha when an eclipse of the sun makes Jayadratha relax his guard; he will kill Karna when Karna struggles to free his chariot wheel that is stuck in the mud.

Kutaja was the son of Bharadvaja, a rishi who appears frequently in Hindu mythology. In Kauṭilya's Arthashasthra, Bharadvaja is frequently cited as the source of a realist attitude to power – how it was to be attained, exercised, increased, and defended. The primary source for Kauṭilya's citations is missing as we have no manuscripts or copies of such works attributable to Bharadvaja. The Arthashasthra cites Bharadvaja behind a façade of moral disapproval, but the options presented are real ones. Kutaja's actions in the Mahabharata are not those of a selfless teacher, but rather of one who desires power, fame, and prosperity, if not wealth – for himself, his family, and his progeny. In that sense, Kutaja follows the advice of his father.

Kutaja's story illustrates another, perhaps less important, point. Kutaja was driven to visit Drupada, in the first place, by the requirements of family life, and the demands of his wife. Kutaja had studied the martial arts, strategy, and the art of war in the academic setting of his father's school and may not have planned a life of service to a single patron. Left to himself, he might have followed in the footsteps of his father and taught the martial arts to whoever came to him. This would have required developing an independent reputation as a teacher with a parade of successful students and referrals from them, and probably would have taken a long time – this prospect was not acceptable to his wife who had just given birth to their son Aswatthama.

However, having visited Drupada and suffered the insults of the king, Kutaja was driven by pride and his desire for revenge to get employment as a teacher with the Kauravas in Hastinapura. The wheel of revenge does not stop by itself and in this case, did not even stop after the Great War. His Kaurava patrons made his life comfortable and, as narrated in this story, even helped him acquire a fiefdom in Northern Panchala; though Kutaja's wife does not drive any further decisions, Kutaja follows through on the commitments he makes to Hastinapura. Having trained the Kauravas and the Pandavas, his reputation was made, and he could have retired to pursue his original goal but that would have entailed a significant change in the life he had chosen and to which he had become accustomed. Ultimately, Kutaja is tied by the chains of obligations he accepted, and, despite having his pre-War advice rejected, fights for the losing side in the Great War.

[3] SUYODHANA & KARNA

In this story, Suyodhana attacks the caste system. The Pandavas support the caste system and use caste to disqualify Karna when he challenges Arjuna to a trial of skill. In the modern world, the Indian caste system is universally condemned and its excesses such as untouchability are illegal. The caste system may or may not have existed at the time of the Great War, or been as rigid as it became in historic time.

The Hindu caste system strikes most liberal-minded people as outrageous and dehumanizing. I have no hesitation in condemning it – it is indeed outrageous and dehumanizing. It is amazing that a system like caste could evolve and could survive for so long. That argues that there must have been environmental conditions that made caste a viable adaptation.

The anthropologist Marvin Harris showed how the caste system worked – it stabilizes the distribution of income and wealth, and makes it possible for the larger population to stay unaware of the standard of living of the upper-most class.

Change, evolutionary or revolutionary, occurred in that privileged class and changes in the "few" made no difference to the "many". A powerless super-majority of citizens did not discriminate between rule by foreign tyrants and rule by local tyrants. The long-term consequence of this unrecognized difference would be that a foreign "colonial" ruler could easily squeeze wealth out of the infrastructure and destroy its capacity for growth.

The story of Karna does not present any evidence of conditions to which caste is an adaptive response. What it does do is show that even from the mythical times portrayed here, there was recognition of the pain, suffering, and sheer unfairness of the caste system. It must give us pause that the ancient Indians did not adopt or evolve a caste system without understanding the consequences and accepting them. The caste system did not develop in a moral vacuum.

The story of Karna is heart-wrenching, for the issue of legitimacy – caste being one aspect – shadows his whole life.

[4] DISARMING EKALAVYA

This is another story about the unfairness of the caste system. In this instance, however, Kutaja, the teacher of the Pandavas, collaborates with Arjuna in enforcing discrimination – Kutaja's demand for Ekalavya's thumb as *guru-dakshina* eliminated him as a competitor to Arjuna[77]. Kutaja had originally rejected Ekalavya (a Nishada) as a pupil because of his low caste.

The Mahabharata does not provide any conclusion to the story of Ekalavya. A son of Ekalavya, who is described as the King of the Nishadas, fights for the Pandavas in the Great War. In other Puranas, Ekalavya and his descendants appear in various roles.

[5] RESPECT FOR ALL

During the twelve years of exile, the Pandavas had many adventures – they encountered strange people and creatures, some of whom they fight and others they befriend. Some of these adventures are by themselves – Arjuna and Bhima are often the protagonists. On one of these adventures, Bhima meets Hanuman.

Bhima does not respect beings that he sees as weaker than himself. The monkey Hanuman, Bhima's half-brother, teaches him a lesson. Usually this story is presented as one of Bhima's adventures – I've tried to move the focus to the lesson that Bhima is taught and that he had never learned before this.

---

[77]There is an amusing appendix to the Ekalavya story reported by Mrinal Sen, the Indian filmmaker, which came to me courtesy of a Mahabharata interest group on the internet. Apparently Mrinal Sen was shooting among the Bhils in Madhya Pradesh and an actor nocked an arrow with thumb and forefinger. A Bhil boy piped up that this was improper as it showed disrespect for Ekalavya. Mrinal Sen was impressed with the tribal boy's knowledge of a story from the Mahabharata and many years later repeated this story to a gathering in France that included an Olympic archery champion. The archer pointed out that all over the world, archers (including South American tribes who had never heard of the Mahabharata) used the index and middle finger and that it made little sense to use the thumb when holding the arrow. Apparently only novices use thumb and forefinger to hold the arrow! The Mahabharata story of Ekalavya being disabled by loss of his thumb is clearly not credible in its extant form. However, unless you wish to be confronted by the argumentative Indian, don't tell that to an Indian!

[6] RIGHTS OF THE FOREST-DWELLER

The point of this story is two-fold – one, it shows that Yudhishthira respects other beings and their rights even when the conflict with his own immediate needs (unlike his brothers); and, two, it highlights Yudhishthira's loyalty and sense of fairness.

THE YAKSHA'S QUESTIONS

The Yaksha's questions shown below and Yudhishthira's responses are based on two translations of "The Book of the Forest" (major book 5 of the Mahabharata) by (1) J. A. B. van Buitenen and (2) Bibek Debroy. I've also consulted the Clay Series translation and P. Lal's transcreation. There are problems with the translations, that go from whatever errors might have crept in to the Sanskrit text, to typos during printing. I should add to these my proclivity to make a leap into the unknowable with the attendant uncertainties.

The interested reader can find many variant translations on the internet, and can judge for themselves. I think that these answers run the range from riddles to metaphysical speculation to brahminical interpolation. A few are questions about psychology, or sociology, or politics. A few may even be considered wisdom about the human condition, but other than a handful of these, the questions represent neither knowledge (defined as that which allows one to accomplish some task) nor wisdom (defined as that which allows one to use knowledge with judgment). Traditionally there are supposed to be a hundred questions, but the critical edition has only seventy-three questions. Yudhishthira answered all of them correctly, that is, as a learned person of that time was expected to.

#	The Yaksha said	Yudhishthira said
1	What causes the sun to rise, and	The Universe makes the sun rise, and
2	what accompanies it?	the Gods accompany it.
3	What makes it set, and	Its Inner Nature (Dharma) makes it set, and
4	what makes it stand still?	in Truth it stands still.
5	How does a person become learned,	By studying revealed knowledge one becomes learned,
6	by what does a person attain to great things,	Inner heat (*drive*?) makes a person become great;
7	how does a person get a supporter, o king,	The firm resolution of a person will provide support,
8	how does a person gain wisdom?	Wisdom is gained by a person who works with experienced people.
9	What is the divine nature (*character*?) of the brahmin,	Seeking self-knowledge is their divine nature,
10	what should they follow as their Dharma (*way of life*);	Their Dharma should be in living simply and economically;
11	what is their human reality,	their human reality is death,
12	what makes them look bad?	complaining makes them look bad.
13	What is the divine nature of the kshatriya,	Seeking weapons is their divine nature,
14	what should they follow as their Dharma?	Their Dharma should be the path of sacrifice;
15	What is their human reality,	their human reality is fear,
16	what makes them look bad?	Desertion (abandoning duty) makes them look bad.
17	Which is the one rhythm of sacrifice,	The breath-of-life is the rhythm of sacrifice,
18	which is the one act of worship in a sacrifice?	Acting from knowledge is the one act of worship in a sacrifice;
19	What is the one act that controls the sacrifice,	The act of speech by itself controls the sacrifice, and
20	what limits the sacrifice?	(it) limits the sacrifice.
21	What is best for the sown,	Rain is best for the sown,
22	what is best for sowing,	Seed is best for sowing,
23	what is best for settling down,	Cattle are best for settling down,
24	what is best for begetting (*harvesting*)?	a son is best for begetting.

#	The Yaksha said	Yudhishthira said
25	Who senses objects, reasons, is honoured in the world, gets respect from all things, and draws breath, but does not live?	Gods, Guests, Dependents, Ancestors, and one's Self – one who does not distribute to these five, draws breath but does not live.
26	What is greater than the earth,	The mother is greater than the earth,
27	what is higher than the sky,	the father is higher than the sky,
28	what is faster than the wind,	the mind is faster than the wind, and
29	what more numerous than grass?	worries are more numerous than grass (or men).
30	What does not close eyes when asleep,	A fish does not close the eyes when asleep,
32	what does not stir when born,	an egg does not stir when born,
33	what has no heart,	a rock has no heart,
34	what grows by speeding along?	a river grows by speeding along.
35	Who is the friend of the traveller,	The caravan is the friend of the traveller,
36	who is the friend at home,	the wife is the friend at home,
37	who is the friend of the sick man,	the physician is the friend of the sick man,
38	who is the friend of a dying person?	Charity is the friend of the dying person.
39	What travels alone,	The sun travels alone,
40	what once born is born again,	the moon is reborn,
41	what is the cure for snow,	fire is the cure of snow,
42	what is the greatest field	the earth is the greatest field.
43	What in one word is (makes) a way of life (Dharma),	Ability/Hard work in one word is a way of life,
44	what in one word is (makes) graciousness,	Charity in one word is graciousness
45	what in one word is (makes) heaven,	Truth in one word is heaven,
46	what in one word is (makes) happiness?	Integrity in one word is happiness.
47	What is the innermost self of a man,	A son is the innermost self of a man,
48	what is the friend made by fate,	a wife is the friend made by fate,
49	what is the support of his life,	the rain-gods are the support of his life,
50	what is a man's final goal?	Charity is his final goal.

#	The Yaksha said	Yudhishthira said
51	What is the best fortune,	Ability is the best fortune,
52	what is the best gift,	Learning is the best gift,
53	what is the most profitable,	Health the most profitable,
54	what may be the best happiness?	Contentment the best happiness.
55	What is the first Law of the world,	Don't be unkind is the first Law,
56	what way of life always bears fruit,	the three-fold way of life always bears fruit,
57	what does not cause grief when tamed,	the mind does not grieve when tamed,
58	what union does not age?	the union of the virtuous does not age.
59	What, when abandoned, increases friendship (*love?*)	Pride, when abandoned, increases friendship,
60	What, when abandoned, will not be grieved,	Anger, when abandoned, will not be grieved,
61	What, when abandoned, increases wealth,	Desire, when abandoned, increases wealth,
62	What, when abandoned, increases happiness?	Greed, when abandoned, increases happiness.
63	what may be death for a man,	Dead is the poor man,
64	how may a kingdom be dead,	dead the kingdom without a king,
65	how may a shraddha be dead,	dead the shraddha performed by the ignorant,
66	how may a sacrifice become dead?	dead the sacrifice with unpaid fees.
67	What is the way (*direction*)?	Asceticism is the way, and
68	What is called water?	the sky is water,
69	What is food? and	the cow is food, and
70	What is poison?	begging is poison;
71	What specifies the time for a shraddha? Then you may take a drink.	A brahmin specifies the right time for a shraddha. What do you think, o Yaksha? (i.e., have I answered your questions correctly, and therefore, may I drink)!

#	The Yaksha said	Yudhishthira said
72	You have answered my questions correctly eliminating all opposition Now tell me exactly who you consider a man, and	When word of a (man's) good deed reaches heaven and earth, then while it stays fresh, (him) I consider a man.
73	who (would you consider) a man who owns all riches.	And that man owns all riches who values equally love and *schadenfreude,* joy and sorrow, the past and the future.

An interesting factoid is that when Alexander invaded India, he had a meeting with a bunch of Indian "philosophers" (possibly he meant "brahmins"), and the questions they asked the scholars who had come with Alexander were very like these questions.

[7] KARNA'S TRAVAILS

On the sixteenth day of the Great War, Karna's wheels get stuck. He puts down his weapons, removes his armour and tries to get it unstuck. When Arjuna threatens to kill him, Karna argues that since he is unarmed, Arjuna should wait so that they could engage in honourable single combat. Krishna ridicules the idea. Then Karna tries to recall the *brahmastra* spell that he had learned from Parashurama. He is unable to recall it. Both these events – his chariot being stuck and his loss of memory at a critical moment – are due to curses directed at him when he went to study with Parashurama disguised as a brahmin.

Karna's search for Knowledge in disguise is a false search. He seeks Power, not Knowledge. In that respect his behaviour contrasts with Yudhishthira's behaviour in the Yakshaprashna episode. This story may have an element of brahminical interpolation in that Karna's search for Power is considered illegitimate. That is a late gloss on the kind of knowledge represented by the Vedas where *mantras* give the priest power over the gods. Knowledge IS power and would be reserved to the brahmins in later times, but in the time of the Mahabharata, even non-brahmins could legitimately seek knowledge. This is just a warning shot.

[8] THE JUDGMENT OF YUDHISHTHIRA

The poet Vyaasa explains that this change was a consequence of the gods assembling at that horrible place. But it would be equally logical to assert that the gods assembled in the places that were pleasant; and in this case, the poet tells us that the reason why the place had turned so pleasant was Yudhishthira's determination to comfort his brothers. Instantly, the gods gathered there, drawn to goodness as moths to a flame.

GLOSSARY OF NAMES

The following table shows how names and words in Sanskrit are spelled out in English (I.e., Roman script), how they should be pronounced, and, for people or places, provides brief sketch of the relationship to the main story.

The Pronunciation column uses a multi-syllabic scheme that I devised. This scheme breaks the Sanskrit word down into a sequence of compound elements containing one or more syllables – these elements are represented by marked-up English words *to be pronounced as they would be in "Standard English"*. Some part of the words or syllables in the element are placed within parentheses to indicate components of the word or syllable should not be expressed. For example, the Sanskrit सुखम्. is pronounced as "soo(t)-come" – the English word "soot", but drop the "t" sound as excess, followed by the word "come". Note that "Sue-come" does not work because the pronunciation of "Sue" in English is equivalent to the Sanskrit सू rather than सु. The use of "come" is a pragmatic compromise – the Sanskrit ख (an aspirated "k") does not occur in English and is usually pronounced as क. This is a problem in the scripts of some Indian languages, such as Tamil, which do not express aspirated phonemes. We apply the principle that anything done to Sanskrit pronunciation in an Indian language can also be done to it in English. Thus सुखम्.becomes सुकम्.in this transliteration for which error I forgive myself.

Sanskrit words/names often end in "a(h)" or in "u(h)" – the first is a long "aa" sound as in "ah" but without the aspirated "h", and the second is the short "a" sound (also called a "schwa" written "ə", an upside-down "e" in the international phonetic script), but also without an aspirated "h".

The international phonetic script remains the gold standard for pronunciation guides; unfortunately, it cannot be read without some education. This make-shift system is an attempt to create something that the ordinary English reader might be able to use without delay and with some degree of confidence that they are pronouncing words correctly.

Glossary of Names (page 1 of 3)

Spelled Name	Guide to Pronunciation	Description in The Greatest War
Amba	(H)um-baa	The eldest of the three Kashi princesses kidnapped by Bhishma as wives for Vichitravirya.
Arjuna	Urge-oon-a(h)	Third son of Pandu and Kunti
Bharata	Burr-a-tuh	Ancestor of Kuru, the dynast of Hastinapura. Son of Shakuntala and Dushyanta
Bharadvaja	Burr-oth(er)-va(h)-ju(h)	Father of Kutaja/Drona.
Bhargava	Bar-gu(h)-vaa(h)	Descendant of Bhrigu, a rishi believed to have composed parts of the Vedas.
Bhima	Beam-u(h)	Second son of Pandu and Kunti
Bhishma	Beesh-mu(d)	Alternate name of Devavrata, the eldest son of Shantanu and "Ganga".
Chitrangada	Chi(ll)-t-ra-(ru)ng-other	Son of Shantanu by Satyavati; crowned King when Santanu dies; dies childless.
Dhaartaraashtra	Thar-th(ick)-ra(h)-shh-tru(h)	A child/descendant of Dhritarashtra
Devavrata	They've-ov(en)-rut	Eldest son of Shantanu by Ganga
Dhritarashtra	Dri(nk)-th(ick)-ra(h)-shh-tru(h)	Weak king, father of Suyodhana and the hundred Kauravas.
Drona	Drone-u(h)	Also called Kutaja – martial arts instructor of Hastinapura

Glossary of Names (page 2 of 3)

Spelled Name	Guide to Pronunciation	Description in The Greatest War
Duryodhana	Th(e)-uri-yo-th(e)-un-u(h)	Also called Suyodhana; son of Dhritarashtra and mortal enemy of the Pandavas
Duhshasana	Dooh-shaw-sun-uh	Brother of Suyodhana; second Kaurava
Dvaipaayana	The-why-pa-yen-u(h)	See "Krishna Dvaipaayana" below
Ganga	Gun-ga(h)	Devavrat's mother
Indraprastha	In-dhruh-prush-thu(s)	Settlement on the Yamuna that becomes the capital city of the Pandavas
Kampilya	Come-pill-yeah	Capital of Panchala
Karna	Cur-nu(h)	Eldest son of Kunti by the Sun, abandoned and raised by a lower-caste family. Good friebd and ally of Suyodhana
Kashi	Kāśi Kaa-she	City on the Ganga
Kaunteya	Kaunteya Cow-n-thé-yu(h)	Male descendant of Kunti
Kaurava	Kaurava Cow-ru(h)-vu(h)	Male descendant of Kuru
Krishna Dvaipaayana	Krish-nu(h) The-why-pa-yen-u(h)	Premarital son of Satyavati by the sage Parashara; fathers Vichitravirya and Chitrangada at his mother's request; also father of Vidura.
Kuru	coup-roo	Ancestor who renames Nagapura to Hastinapura and begins the ruling dynasty of the city.

Glossary of Names (page 3 of 3)

Spelled Name	Guide to Pronunciation	Description in The Greatest War
Kutaja	coot-a-ju(h)	Name of Drona, the martial arts teacher of Hastinapura
Khandavaprastha	Khan-dove-a-pruss-ta	Barren lands south-west of Hastinapura that became prosperous after the establishment of Indraprastha.
Panchala	Paan-chaal-u(h)	Kingdom ruled by Drupada, south of Hastinapura on the Ganga; Prays for a son who would kill Kutaja/Drona and gets a son and daughter. That daughter is Krishnaa, also called Draupadi, who marries the five Pandavas and whose public assault and humiliation motivate the war.
Panchali	Paan-chaal-lee	Daughter of Pancala, used for Draupadi.
Pandava	Pa-unde(r)-vu(h)	Sons of Pandu by Kunti and Madri.
Pandu	Pa-unde(r)-oo	Second son of Vichitravirya who becomes king because his older brother is blind; Father of the Pandavas/
Shantanu	Shawn-ton-oo	Father of Devavrat by Ganga; marries Satyavati; father of Chitrangada and Vichitravirya.
Suyodana	Sue-yo-the-nu(h)	Also called Duryodhana. Mortal enemy of Pandavas; eldest son of Dhritarashtra; leader of the Kauravas.
Vichitravirya	Which-it-ru(h)-vee-ryu(h)	Son of Shantanu by Satyavati; marries Ambika and Ambalika; dies childless
Yudhishthira	You-dish-tea-ru(h)	The oldest Pandava and the future King of Hastinapura